HONEYWOOD

ALSO BY DARRELL KINSEY

Torsino

HONEYWOOD

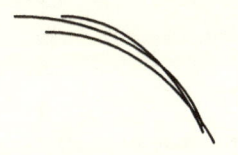

DARRELL KINSEY

A BEVELED MIRROR BOOK
Published by Kinsey Publishing
131 East Broad Street
Number 205
Athens, Georgia 30601

ISBN 978-0-615-24465-5

to Loudelle

Kyle sat wrong in the wicker chair. His black work shoes, streaked with white saltwater stains, sank down in the stuffed seat cushion, and the chair's high back supported him across the buttoned back pockets of his pants. The condo was cool with air conditioning. Maunar's maid cart propped the front door open, and humidity condensed in beads on the white tile floor. The beach outside burned bright through the sliding glass doors behind him, and the harbor water looked like melted glass through the dark palm fronds. He leaned forward with his elbows on his knees, staring down, gone in mind from the condominium he was in and thinking deep in his head with pictures that were dredged by the makeup-colored background of the seat cushion. His daydreams were of the femininity he had known back home. Steam, billowing out from behind Julie's shower curtain, rolled towards a slipstream that a rattling exhaust fan sucked through a ceiling case, and her blond hair was always dark orange when wet, the clumps coiled on her sun-freckled shoulders and tank top straps, and a straightening iron always warmed on the countertop next to a nest of tubes and cases and products. She would sing with the stereo that played from the upstairs living room. Shuffled memories came from all directions, like the memories from childhood when he saw and heard without really understanding the situations of his witness. He went back further in time. His mother rarely dressed, preferring home and the airiness of nightgowns over parties and the confines of underwear. When she did dress, the household air was different. Green streaks of fabric paint across the chair cushion brought him back into the condo. Strokes of kelly and mint made modern art palm fronds across the seat cushion, but there were real palm fronds outside. He got the idea to turn and look at them, but the trance was slow to fade. He couldn't make himself move his head. The stare felt good and was hard to break out of. He forced himself to blink. He turned around to look through the sliding glass doors behind him. Hanging from the balcony above, the bold rainbow colors of a whirligig spiraled and drilled in the air, and the palm fronds reared against the wind like the shaking heads of bothered horses. Jostled shadows scanned across the narrow yard of beach below. Iguanas kicked in the sand trying to find consistent patches of sunlight that weren't too far away from their refuge stand of smooth palm trunks, and the harbor water shimmered in the sun. Maunar's image showed up. Her figure in the baby blue maid's uniform reflected in the sliding door and superimposed on the view. Kyle turned and faced forward again. He climbed down to sit right in the wicker chair.

Maunar tucked a loose arc of wiry hair in with the others. She leaned over cleaning the glass top of the coffee table. A copper mermaid supported the pane with her back. The statue leaned forward like a figurehead. The face was cute, and the mermaid didn't wear a shirt. Hanging from her torso, her breast had a realistic look of moveable weight, but they were frozen in metal and patina-ridden, and her tail was stuck in the middle of a violent whip like a fried catfish whose muscles shrank to its skeleton during a final turn in hot grease. Maunar sprayed soap foam on the glass and wiped it clean. She arranged everything back. Buttons of the universal remote were primary and bone colored, and Maunar eased a vase down onto the clean glass. Paper flowers and sticks fountained out of the top, and Maunar fanned the magazines across the table. Downy ends of an ornamental switch stuck up from the centerpiece, and tufts brushed across her black cheek while she worked. She didn't pay attention to it or touch her face after she stood up straight, and the mermaid carried the spread again. Maunar studied the arrangement of items, patting her hair. One of the magazines had been wrinkled and torn by the guests. She slid it out of the fan, respaced the gap it left and tucked it under her arm, the glossy cover next to the baby blue rayon of her uniform sleeve.

"Are you going to steal that magazine?" Kyle said.

"I'm going to steal your mind. Don't you have your own work?"

Maunar slung the damp white towel over her shoulder and walked down the hall toward the open front door, propped by her maid's cart. Floor tiles threw back the outside. Maunar walked on the light and lost all of her own color in the glare. She was a black figure, silhouetted. She walked slow, switching her hips back and forth and letting her spray bottle dangle at her side from one finger. Kyle stood up and followed her.

She unfolded the torn magazine and looked at the cover. The tear stretched across the hot pink letters of the nameplate and ended up as a white lightning bolt on the cover girl's forehead. Maunar read the teasers on the front in a mumble to herself, and her lips moved. Kyle leaned against her cart and touched the propped door with his palm. The metal held the sun's morning heat, and the burning feeling came to his palm all at once. He jerked his hand back.

"I guess I won't report the theft," he said.

"Nobody cares if I take this magazine," she said. She bent over and put it under a stack of clean towels on the bottom rack of her cart. "I might enjoy looking at that tonight while I soak myself in a bubble bath."

"If nobody cares, why are you hiding it under those towels?"

"Stop now. I have work to do."

She carried a stack of clean white sheets down the hall and turned into the master bedroom. The curtains were drawn. Maunar threw her hooked finger at the switchplate, and the globe below the ceiling fan came on dim and sickly compared to the outside light that shone through the threads of the drawn curtains. The queen bed was unmade. Sheets lay swirled in the center, and the floral comforter hung off the foot. Blades in the ceiling fan started slow turns, and under the alarm clock on the nightstand, a corner of folded tip money stuck out. Maunar counted the corners without unfolding the bills. "Nice people," she said. "They were from Canada. Spoke French sometimes."

Kyle sat in an armchair in the corner of the room below the window. He watched her stuff the money in the pentagon-shaped pocket at her pelvic bone. "Don't look at my money," she said. "You might start getting thirsty for a cold beer that I'm not planning to buy for you. Bubble bath night is getting alright looking. Might be a bottle of white wine on the bathmat next to the tub. You never know. You just never do know."

Kyle smiled.

"Be quiet and hold these and be honest," Maunar said, and she threw the stack of clean sheets at him. "And don't picture me in a bubble bath." The sheets unfolded in the air and landed in his lap. She stripped the bed down, jerking the elastic mittens of the bottom sheet out from under the corners they covered and piled all the bedclothes in the center of the bare metallic-blue mattress. She bent over and hugged the wad against her chest and stood up. The comforter fell to the carpet, and Maunar kicked past it walking around the bed and out into the hall with the dirty sheets.

The blades still spun at an easy speed, and the fan was on a low setting. Kyle looked around the room. In the folds of the comforter, he saw a pair of tortoiseshell sunglasses. He leaned over and picked them up, and Maunar came in again. "Where did you get those?" she said.

"What?"

"The sunglasses. Those aren't yours. Those are that man's. Where were they?"

"In the comforter."

"You have to run up to the lobby and see if they're still here. You have to give them back."

"I don't know. These look pretty nice," Kyle said. He unfolded the brindle ear blades, and scrawled signatures were etched into little gold plaques next to the hinges on each side. "What name is this? Is it a designer? Have you ever seen this logo in any of your magazines?"

"No, you better not. You better not say that I'm stealing magazines, so you can steal sunglasses. Ernest doesn't want trashed up magazines on the table, and magazines and expensive glasses are different stories anyway. Have you ever thought they could be prescription?"

Kyle held the lenses up to the light coming through the curtains. "They aren't prescription," he said.

"You better get to that lobby right now. That man's wife was all over him about those glasses all week, making sure he still had them. Run. Go up there now."

Kyle stretched his arms above his head with the glasses in his hand. "Run," she said. "I'm not kidding. Don't act like you're stretching. Get going."

"I'm going."

Outside and then semi-outside, his foot sounds bounced in the concrete stairwell at the end of the building, and in the covered walk, the bladed light hit in the corner of his eye between scorched stucco columns. He held the glasses in his hand. He didn't run. He walked fast, lit and unlit in the tropical light and burning gold heat. He walked in the shadows of the roofs and canopies, but the sun filled crevices and baked them, and he felt heat from the ball of fire on different parts of his body while he walked. It was hot in an instant and gone, and the planet bulged out into space in the tropics. The sun beat down on the huge wild leaves of a banana tree. A column of light found an orange and black beetle in the folds of a flaming flower, and it found Kyle's fingernails when he swung his arm walking into an open space of the portico. The top of his head and his shoulder lit up going around someone's suitcase parked in the middle of the walkway on built-in wheels. He kicked through the gravel in the courtyard and ducked under hanging crab claw blooms. A pebble clicked across the bricks to the surface of a phosphorescent fountain pool. Dark expensive rooms in the shade had porches that opened to the gardens. They grew like domestic jungles, and a faucet with a blue wheel hissed, and a curtain of slow leak water hugged the wall and drained down a stain. A hose gagged its spigot at the nozzle and led off into leathery bushes. The sprinkler lay hidden in the leaves, and the spray it threw up disappeared into a prism and evaporated in the air before having a chance to fall back down on the orders of plants below. Burgundy tubes curled. A man sat with his foot propped on the wooden rail outside his room. He read the complimentary newspaper he found at his door, the pages stretched in front of his face and chest. His juice glass sat next to his chair legs on the terra cotta, full of juice. Stepping stones under Kyle's feet rocked in their cradles of damp black earth, and the man let a corner of the newspaper page go limp. Kyle saw his face and nodded. The man nodded and snapped the page stiff again, covering himself. Two rooms down, the front door was left open, and the view through the suite was shotgun through to a late brunch party on the harbor-side porch. The silhouetted heads talked, and a ponytail whipped around in conversation. The barrette that it stemmed from looked like it had landed there and might take off again soon, and Kyle walked on through the different add-ons of the hotel. They got older the closer he got to the lobby, and the smell of history grew rich. The renovated carriage house. The smoke house had been converted into guest quarters, and the buildings were the elements and minerals of the old island, a midden reformed in stacks and piles, and the steadfast materials commingled with the modern people it now housed. The hotel clamped down its plot of land but represented it, the arches' plaster of native sand and lime held banded gray seashells, and beams of blanched driftwood supported the loggia's ceiling. The quindecagon ballroom had fifteen french doors, one on each wall. All were open, and Kyle took a shortcut onto the empty dance floor looking up into the painted dome ceiling and sprawling iron chandelier. Douglas, an old black janitor, had mopped half the floor, and Kyle walked around the shining wet places and threw his hand up to him. Douglas nodded and looked down again, drumming the palm-side of his knuckles against the mop handle. Kyle left on the opposite side he came in on. He used his skeleton swipe card to get through a wrought-iron gate. The little light by the sensor changed from red to green, and he heard the bolt slide back mechanically. Pruned oleander lined the winding brick path that opened into one of the private courtyards. Two girls sunned facedown on collapsed-back chaise lounges, the straps of their bikini tops, bright yellow and cigar brown, hung untied on the brickwork, and Kyle saw their white sides and pale underarms. The Rolling Stones played through a black boom box, and a lizard stood at the edge of the brick looking at the little stereo and twisting its head. Kyle slipped into the bushes unnoticed and turned sideways through a narrow gap between a brick wall and a stucco wall. He came out in the service alley behind the kitchen. A marginal time of late morning when some wanted lunch but others still wanted breakfast, he smelled pancakes and hamburgers. He still heard the girls' music but only because he knew it was there. Other sounds came from the kitchen through the screen door, water hitting metal and pots clanging. Murals covered the cement block wall. Old frescos of saints faded near more modern work. Bruno, the head cook, slipped out to paint sometimes. Cartoon Rastafarians slumped with half-lidded eyes, and black quarter notes hovered above their braids. Painted one Transfer Day, red and white stripes engulfed a blue field, and representing the mother country, Bruno glued fifty dried starfish to the blue section. Kyle recognized the children sitting on the ground as server's children, and the little boy made a dirty doll ride naked on the back of a stuffed dinosaur. The little girl hummed and made sound effects with her mouth, narrating the imagined journey and laughing. Her braids shook and bobbed, and the plastic balls that tied them off tapped against each other. Kyle stepped over their play and went in the back door of the main building. Down a corridor toward the lobby, pink and black tiles hung on the walls and flanked a mosaic of sailboats at sunset.

The lobby was a wide room with an old ceiling supported by rich wooden beams hewn from soldier trees, and looking through the automatic glass doors, no cab was pulled under the porte-cochere and no one waited there with luggage. Only Manny paced in the shade wearing his bellhop uniform and smoking a cigarette.

A tall man wore linen pants that moved like toilet paper. He leaned over the back of a woman using a laptop on the fall front of a tall secretary. An airline's website showed on the screen.

"Excuse me. Sorry. Have you just checked out?" Kyle said.

"No, not until tomorrow."

Maria sat behind the counter helping a family of three, father, mother and a little girl with bright red curls. "Excuse me, are yall checking out?" Kyle said to the father.

"They're checking in," Maria said.

The brass elevator doors opened, and a man in a black suit with slicked-back hair came out power-walking across the lobby with dress shoes resounding off the marble floor. Kyle caught up with him. "Sir, excuse me, sir. Have you by any chance just checked out?"

"I'm not even a guest. I'm just visiting. Thank you anyway," he said and kept walking. The glass doors slid open for him and also for Manny who came into the lobby from outside, smoke still floating out of his mouth. Manny walked toward Kyle, his salt and pepper beard messed up and his eyes red in his weathered face.

"There he is," Manny said.

"Who?" Kyle said.

"You, partner. There you are." Manny grabbed Kyle's arm and squeezed it and smiled and let out a gruff laugh.

"Manny?"

"Hey hey," he said.

"Have you seen any Canadians today?"

"These people who just left seemed northern, yeah. Wait a minute. You're not from up north anywhere are you?"

"No, Georgia."

"Okay, I'm Louisiana. I don't know about Canada. They just told the cabbie to go to the airport," Manny said and laughed. "First things first." His laugh turned into a cough, and he put the cuff of his bellhop jacket up to his mouth, the sleeve piped with braided gold rope. Manny slapped Kyle in the back, and his own choking improved.

"Are you alright?" Kyle said.

"Yeah, I'm coughing."

"And your eyes are a little red."

Tiles of darker marble formed radials that led to the center of the lobby. An urn made of volcanic ash held flowers, vines and twisting sticks. It sat on an oval table under a mirror that hung between ceiling beams facing down towards the wilds of the tall arrangement. Manny leaned over the table. The plants of the centerpiece touched his face, and he looked up at his reflection. He made a face. He stuck his lower jaw out and pulled down the bottom lids of his eyes. "Yeah, I might have done myself in a little last night," he said. "Hey let me get over here and check on this."

He walked over to the family at the counter. Maria had just finished checking them in, and the father was bending over to reach the handle of his suitcase. Manny got to the handle first, and the father let him pick up all of their bags, the navy and burgundy adult cases, and Manny put his arm through the strap of the little girl's bumblebee knapsack. He led them across the lobby and raised his eyebrows passing Kyle. The family followed him to the brass elevator doors. Manny reached out for the elevator's call button, but the little girl with red curls ran over. "I want to do it," she said, and the button lit up under her small finger.

"She loves to press buttons," her mother said.

"Oh yeah, I used to, too. It can be fun until you wake up one day and find yourself divorced," Manny said. The couple chuckled and looked up at the row of numbers above the brass doors. The little girl clapped and stomped the polished floor. She looked up at each parent and pressed the up button again. It stayed lit.

"Don't do that, sweetie. Look it's already all lit up. That means the elevator already knows we're down here waiting," her mother said, and the brass pane of elevator doors took their reflection, blurred and warm like a psychedelic portrait, family plus bellhop shining in lacquer like a horn's, and Kyle walked down the hall past the counter. He pulled the sunglasses out of his pocket and studied them while he walked. The tortoiseshell frames were see-through in parts, and the reddish and amber specks glowed in the sconce lamplight of the hall. A gold strip ran across the top of the frames and across the bridge and melded with the plaque where the designer's signature was etched. They looked expensive, and coming to the heavy door at the end of the hall, he stopped and put them on. He walked through the door and into the lounge, now tobacco-tinted, and he slowed his walk and put his hands in the pockets of his khaki work pants. Feeling magnified and commanding, he held himself up straight, moving with the music the bartender played through cabinet speakers on each side of the mirror-backed shelves. Square bottles held honey-colored liquor. Men in swimsuits sat shirtless, leaning forward with their forearms on the leather bar padding. Even half naked, the men looked expensive, and their skin glowed rich with the absorption of sunlight. Their bodies brought in an element of outside to the dark room. They drank early and watched a flat screen, and the high definition tennis match was dulled for Kyle under the influence of the lenses. The television was muted. The men read closed caption bars that scrolled across the bottom of the screen, and the low-cropped grass had been worn down around the baseline. The ceiling fans were set to spin on high. Their motors rocked, and the blades spun invisible, sending air down through the silver hair of the men, lifting the wisps that weren't matted down damp or chlorine-stiffened, and Kyle kept walking through, seeing everyone in the lounge and looking straight at everyone's face with the protection of the sunglasses. By the unused fireplace, members of a group spread out on the low couches and the painted bricks of the wide hearth. The women in the group wore hard faces, strong jaws and haircuts of power, their exercised bodies wood-carved and slight in their sundresses and pedal pushers. One asserted a nearly finished glass of vodka and melted ice while she talked. "We need drinks. We need big drinks."

"It's not lunch time."

"I know. It's drink time!" someone said, and they all laughed.

"Do you like bourbon at all?"

"It doesn't matter just as long as it's a drink. No, I'm just kidding. I don't mean to sound like I'm sounding, but just a shot of something please." They all laughed again. "We're on vacation. Hey, we're on serious vacay time."

Outside was aged and discolored. Everything was shaded sepia and cream and beige and brown and amber through the designer glasses. The sun was a buff disc the color of dishwater. Everything looked wooden like the inlays of an intarsia, and the splintered rays of the sun polarized into rods across the sky. The pool water was old serum in a medicine bottle. Across the deck at the balustrade, he overlooked the beach where the shallow water frothed like a pilsner, skating across the slick, flat sand around the ankles of combers and farther out, around the waists of waders. Beyond the two shoulders of mountain that swept down to hug the harbor separate from the true sea, the water got darker, a burgundy molasses. He never wore sunglasses. He took them off, and the mountains, the water, his hands returned to the colors he knew them to be under the natural light of the sun, the riotous hyper-colors of the vibrant tropics, and the sun still hung like it always had, blasting a white hole in the blue of sky. He looked at it, and his colored iris muscles flexed and reduced his pupil to the size of a period in print. The eye needed exercise, too, he thought, and he didn't know what to do with the sunglasses. Their owner was gone, and he didn't want them like he thought he had. He put them in his pocket.

June, the beginning of hurricane season, they had to cut the coconuts from the palm tops, or in high winds, they would fly as cannon shells against the windows and glass doors of the hotel. Don wore the same baby blue knit polo and khakis that was Kyle's uniform, and Kyle followed him across the beach into the shade of the fronds carrying an aluminum ladder under his arm.

Kyle put the legs into the sand and uncoupled the ladder at the side, extending it to rest the top rung against the smooth palm bark. A bumper sticker of slanted yellow and black caution bars stuck to the aluminum, and so did diagrams showing red stickmen who used the ladder in hazardous ways. Lightning bolts happened at their injuries, and Don pulled the machete out. He dropped its green canvas sheath in the sand and started climbing. Kyle watched the legs of the ladder sink into the sand under his weight, and Kyle steadied the ladder, leaning forward and putting both hands on the sides like gripping the shoulders of someone who needed to be leveled with. Don swung into the fronds, and husked coconuts dropped into the sand like meteorites in their green-splotched cases. He hung on the trunk and swung around, keeping one foot on the ladder and making strikes at the backside of the tree. Two more coconuts thudded in the sand, and Don backed down the ladder throwing the machete blade into the ground from halfway up. He jumped off the ladder and pulled the machete out of the sand. Holding the sides of the blade under the hood of his black hand, he offered Kyle the handle end. "Do you want to try the next one?" he said.

Kyle took the handle.

Two palms stood together, both arching toward the water, and a brunette with blond highlights sat in the hemp hammock that stretched between them. White wires led into her ears, and she read a paperback. Seeing them coming toward her with the ladder, she closed the book around her index finger and pulled on one of the wires so that an earbud popped out and fell on her chest above the floral one-piece that covered her. "Do I need to move?" she said.

"He's just a beginner, but this tree looks empty and that one curves out that way, so please keep relaxing," Don said. "Don't worry about him."

Kyle climbed the ladder to the top of the tree and swung at the closest coconut. The blade missed the point of attachment and hit in the case, lodging inside. He jerked to bring the metal out of the husk, and threads followed it. A knot of coarse fibers hung from the side of the wounded coconut, and he swung again and missed into the pile of fronds. They rattled and continued rattling after the blow was through. The lavender tail of an iguana whipped out of its nest in the tree's topknot. Kyle saw the tips of its dewlap, and its black spike ends moved down the tree on the opposite side of the trunk. Kyle looked down at the woman. She read again with her earbud restored, and Don saw what happened and backed away from the ladder to give the lizard space. It spiraled down the tree popping the trunk skin with its claws. It stopped and stood still on the hammock rope where it was tied around the tree, and from its cabriole foot, black razors came out of its scaly gaiter and curled around the double knot. The iguana was frozen and staring at the woman. It was a dinosaur, wrinkled with elderly genes and a tired expression like it had inherited dawn-of-time memories from its ancestors, and their collected experiences included everything that had ever gone on. The iguana had seen this before, a resting woman unaware of its presence, and it sat prepared for her reaction to pure hideousness. She looked up over the top of her book and saw the iguana. She put the paperback down by her thigh, eased out of the hammock and squatted in the sand beside a sequined beach bag that held her things. The hammock had pressed diamonds into the skin of her leg backs, and from under a folded towel on top, she brought out a camera with an elongated snout of lens. She uncapped the front, put the viewfinder to her unsquinted eye and made adjustments to the long cylinder by twisting it. Arcs of purple and blue and white light rotated around the surface of the outer lens. The shutter whispered in the core of the camera, and the iguana seemed unimpressed. It had seen tourism, too, and it walked down the trunk onto the sand, trudging through it by rotating its ghostly joints bent at right angles.

In the maids' break room, Kyle faced the warm red curvature of a drink machine. The wet bottle stood on the pinnacle of an ice mound like an armless Cristo Redentor. Slush clung to its sides, and a spenserian script was rotated sideways. He straightened a dollar and fed it into the slot, and the insides grumbled with mechanical digestion. A can of Coke dropped into the black tray and rocked. "What kind do you want, Don? My treat."

Maids sat in metal chairs around the folding table, their places set with cracker wrappers and microwaveable trays and wrinkled displays of sauce-covered tinfoil. Don put the machete down on the paper veneer of the folding table and leaned over Maunar, his face in the crook of her neck, whispering into her skin. She laughed and played and pushed at his head and sat up away from him, swaying her back and straightening the paper towel placemat under her sliced nectarines. Kyle fed another dollar into the machine, ran his fist into the oversized button, and a Sprite fell into the black tray and rocked back and forth. Both cans perspired in his hand, and he put the Sprite on the folding table and opened his Coke. Gases hissed from under the tab, and he levered the shield-shaped section of aluminum into the can and through the surface of the dark liquid. He drank it. The bubbles fizzed against the roof of his mouth and hit the back of his throat, burning it. Foam sizzled in the can when he took it away from his mouth, and he heard the drink leaping from itself and hitting against the aluminum interior.

Don stood up from Maunar. "We need to get the wheelbarrow," he said, picking up the machete from the top of the folding table.

"Warriors who battle the dreaded coconut," Maunar said. The maids erupted.

"You laugh, but they're guarded by ferocious iguanas. Ask Kyle. It's not the chest of gold but the pirate's sword that stings."

"Profound jackass," Maunar mumbled and grinned, and Della, the big maid at the table's head, shook all over. Her cheeks balled and glowed like radioactive berries, and her eyes turned into slits of cloven brown skin like coffee beans.

"She said something disrespectful, but we'll just ignore it," Don said to Kyle. "We'll be mature and walk away to our work." He headed toward the door. Kyle picked up the unopened Sprite and pointed it toward Don who disappeared into the hall of painted concrete block. He left the can on the table in front of Della, and she leaned back in her chair laughing.

They heard the maids laughing and talking until going through the metal door that led to the stairwell. "We have the time of my life together," Don said. "She's a natural rascal, Maunar, don't you think?"

In the basement, the utility lights hung on the wall in wire cages fed by silver cables that ran along the ceiling. Don picked up the handles of the overturned wheelbarrow and crossed his arms to guide the bed over like leading a ballroom partner through a turn. The inflated tire pivoted in place on the grit of the sandy concrete floor, and once righted and facing the exit, Don went forward with it. Kyle pushed open the double doors, and the painted planks swung out into the daylight wobbling on old hinges whose emblazoned rust broke through an old film of white paint. In the shade of the building, the older maids leaned back against the wall sitting on a low wooden bench. Josephine, the lead maid, hugged all day by her vest, sat talking, and sun-spotted Bonnie pinched tobacco from her breast pocket and rolled a cigarette and licked the paper. Grace, already smoking, sent rotating wisps of gray smoke through the shaded air. They floated into the sun and turned blue. Don and Kyle crossed the shade line. The demarcation scanned them, and their faces went into squints. They acknowledged the ladies who nodded back.

Don steered the wheelbarrow through the sand, stopping at the coconuts. Kyle picked them up and dropped them gonging in the metal bed. The pile grew and the botanical noggins thudded deep and hollow against each other, and he stacked them into a pyramid. They made one trip, dumped the load and then came back across the crescent of beach with an empty bed to pick up the rest, following a similar route but making a third line of tread tracks in the white sand all the way to the other end where the three pariah palms stood in huddle near the sudden rise of dark lush mountain slope.

Back in the middle of the beach, two boys came out of the harbor dripping through the sand, carrying foam boogie boards under their arms. They crossed the three tracks in the sand, and one stepped on a track destroying the tread negative and replacing it with the same smooth-sided depressions that were made all over the beach by the heels and big joints of bare feet. The other boy looked down and saw the wheelbarrow marks. "Somebody's been riding a big unicycle through here," he said, and in the sun, they put the rough white sides of their boards down in the sand and sat on the loud colors of the decorated sides. Only small waves broke in the harbor, and they had only floated on their stomachs without much to ride. The sloping mountains took the brunt of the sea shoves, and all that got to the harbor beach was the idea of a wave, the water doubling back on itself, a sucking, a short fall of foam that dumped over and slid across the flat, packed sand, stretching out clear and losing its push to stall out in an arc of water. "That was sort of boring," one boy said, wiping his face. He pulled at his yellow wrist strap, and the mated textures of velcro issued distorted scratches against the unwrapping.

Kyle and Don came back down the beach with another full load of coconuts. The boys saw them coming, and they watched, saluting to have their eyes in their hands' shade.

"Can we have a watermelon?"

"I don't have any watermelons," Kyle said.

"Dude, you got like thirty of them."

"These aren't watermelons."

"I'll give you a hint," Don said. "They came from the trees behind you."

The boys turned, and their wet hair whipped. "They look like palm trees, but I guess they're watermelon trees," the boy said, and both of them laughed together, and one forearmed the other, and they shook their heads and moved wet hair out of their faces.

"Follow me," Don said. He turned the wheelbarrow and pushed it up into the shade parking it beside a concrete picnic table. The boys stood up and followed Don and Kyle dragging their boogie boards through the sand by their rubber coated wrist leashes. Don steadied a coconut on the concrete slab. Overall a pistachio shape, a green cat eye, the ends of the coconut tapered into clumped knots separated by cleaves. Kyle passed Don the machete, and the boys' eyebrows rose with the blade out. They stood staring, awkward-jawed, braces glinting in their dark mouths. They were in the years when hormones changed their bodies and pulled at different parts at different times, puffing their faces up and reddening their cheeks. Kyle looked at them and remembered the same stage, their pale nipples flush with their chests and the whole torso in limbo between the convex bird look of boys and the weighty defined look of men who carry whole cuts of steak in their hairy chests. The boys' shoulders were on the verge of broadening, and their shoulders hoisted them. They were neither slack nor stretched against their frames, and they didn't know how to hold themselves, growing all the time and changing every day. Don split the coconut. Like something pregnant, it first birthed a wash that spread out over the concrete tabletop. Don wrenched the blade in the hard shell, and the clean white meat appeared in halves, sitting on top of its dusty manger of fibrous coir. "So it's a coconut."

"Can we have some?"

They each took a bowl and banged and bit, separating the meat from its shell and cracking it into parts against the concrete. The flesh was dirtied with flecks of plant trash. They touched the particles, and the trash stuck to their fingertips and was gone from the food. They gnawed where it was clean. Their front teeth dragged the surface and shaved the top layers off into their mouths. Don picked through the fibers of the disheveled husk and pulled out a length for each boy, stretching them in turn and testing their durability. "And these," he said, "you can make a necklace from. Just find some seashells with holes, and there's nature's jewelry."

The milk formed streams on the gritty tabletop and flowed toward the slab's edge. Sunlit drips fired down into the sand like tracer bullets, pattering dryly. Then they came faster and collected, tiny bays in the sand, filling up one divot and crawling into the next, moving toward the sea but never getting there. The sand absorbed too well. It was too willing to clump darkly, but the milk was unfit for the sea anyway, even for mingling with the harbor waters,

Kyle thought. He took a broken piece of coconut and chewed the meat away from the shell. He watched the spilled coconut milk, and he thought about it, born to moisten in the private world of the coco sphere, the milk, once released, was finished. The milk couldn't get to the sea, and the milk couldn't hack it in the sea, an aromatic oil swirl in the burning saline. Disaster rolls from the sea, and it drags at the land and heels of man, trying to reclaim what it once gave. God wouldn't put the sea here again because of all the trouble it has caused, a casserole of violence steaming with storms that drive reckless rain through our temples and spreads. Breathed by lobes of bloody gill, the milk couldn't go it, the brainless tendrils groping all, sinking into a dark zone of hardware-headed beasts and see-through creatures with glowing guts, and down and down to where the blackness is reminiscent of nothing. Space has its stars, but the sea is empty until it touches the burning canopies of the underworld. The milk had it easy. Had it not been spilled, its fruit would have one day sucked it back in, and it would be itself again, never having been out of its shell, still white. The sea puts out. The sea smells like fish. As amniotic fluid for the world, the sea has been around, and both good and bad are born in its shallows. Both demons and saints wake up wet. The sea gives and takes away and buffers us from hell. The hardest water, the sea was never meant to be sweet. God would make the coconut again, he thought.

Don and Kyle left the boys with their pieces to eat. They pushed the wheelbarrow through the winding back alleys of the hotel, by the warm metal doors of service entrances and through the row of staff quarters where some of the young summer employees, off work, sat along the walls and in bark littered plots of measly shrubs and dry birdbaths. Midge from Oklahoma tried to play the guitar. She stopped when the coconut load paraded through. Then she went back to staring at the fret board and cracking her knuckles. Two guys took turns throwing the pink and blue Nerf through a hole in the broken latticework of an unpainted gazebo. On the road, they turned right toward the cul de sac where the big metal dumpster sat backed into the foliage under the meshy shade of a mimosa. Kyle slid the door open, and the metal screeched. Together, they lifted the wheelbarrow, and the coconuts tumbled inside with the other coconuts and the trash bags that had been there already.

In the alley at dusk, Kyle and Don helped the musicians bring their equipment to the bandshell. Kyle pulled the thigh of his khakis up and climbed into the back of the moving van. The bass drum's outer head was painted with a crude dragon throwing up flames, and the band's name encircled it in a wreath of letters, The Pan Dragons. He picked up the bass drum, held the shell against his chest and walked to the edge of the moving van. He threw his left ear down to his shoulder and his right ear down to the other shoulder, jerking his head around the drum to see his feet and then jump down into the alley behind the bandshell.

Kyle walked out on stage with the drum. On the lower tier, people sat for dusk dinner. Laminated triptychs of menu concealed their faces on the patio, and the sun and sea acted together in an unnoticed play of sparkles on the surface of the harbor. Settings of cubit zirconium and tombac floated. The musicians hooked themselves up. Ernest, the hotel manager and band leader, stood at the front adjusting the microphone stand. Facing the sea breeze, his yellow shirt with red leaves ballooned in the back. Kyle put the bass drum down on the drummer's platform, and the drummer came in kneeling at it with a black duffel bag. He pulled out the pedal and club mechanism and put it down next to the drum, testing its movements so the mallet would hit in a reinforced circle where all the scuff marks showed it had hit many times before. The steel drummer held his hands inside his shining basin, warming up with half swings at low volume, and the guitar players paced and circled, testing their playing space and stepping over cords that led back to their stack of amps. Red power lights glowed in the twilight. The quartersphere of bandshell was painted the same colors as the banded sunset sky, and in the gap between the mountains, the circumstances of its imitation were coming about.

Don walked up the short staircase at the back of the bandshell uncoiling an orange extension cord. He led it to the keyboardist who was already benched and running his fingers along the plastic keys even though no electricity ran through his instrument. He stopped playing when Don came connecting the trinity of prongs with their holes in the power strip. Now that sound could come out, the keyboardist was shy and sat up straight on his bench. He put his palms on his kidneys and leaned back stretching.

"I think we're through for the day," Don said walking up to Kyle.

"It feels like we should be."

"We are."

They walked down the back steps behind the bandshell together. To the left on the upper tier of the back deck, the waiters filed from double doors, lining up with trays of red drinks. "Good evening," Ernest said into the microphone," his voice deep and warm. Light applause lifted into the wind coming off the harbor.

"Are they any good?" Kyle said.

"Who?"

"The Pan Dragons."

"Yeah, they're not too bad."

Heavier applause came when Ernest announced free rum drinks for everyone. The waiters moved down the steps to the lower tier, and Ernest kept talking into the microphone, his voice amplified and bouncing between the buildings of the hotel. The band played bits of music separate from each other, trying their individual sounds. The keyboardist ran up a scale. "My name is Ernest. I'm the hotel manager slash band leader. We're the Pan Dragons, and it's a special day. Friday is a special day every week here at the Hidden Harbor Resort." Kyle and Don walked down the alley following the empty moving van. Its brake lights came on and went off again, and it inched down the alley, the driver cautious not to scrape its side mirrors on the stucco walls. They slowed down to a walk of procession, their faces red in the brake lights and then dark with the streaked bright sky behind them. The music started. It bounced between the alley walls, muddled like it came from underwater, and kids of staff members, some barefoot and some shirtless, ran laughing past Kyle and Don. They jumped in through the open back door of the moving van. One did a cartwheel, and they jumped and screamed inside the big box of truck. Then they all hopped out and tore back down the alley again, chasing each other and running in the same direction they had come from. Don kept walking through the major corridor, following the van, and Kyle turned left through the buildings toward the staff quarters and his room. "See you tomorrow?" Don yelled.

Kyle turned and walked backwards. "Not tomorrow or the next. Got two days off."

"A good man. I work in the afternoon only. What are you going to do?"

"Roam around, see more of your island."

"Yeah, go see the hospital where I was born. I'm working on getting a plaque hung by the very delivery room. Goodnight."

"Night."

A panel of utility meters wheezed on the wall. Propped mops dried for the next day, and a cat crossed high-shouldered. It jumped on a humming window unit, hooked its paw, licked it and jumped off again. Kyle walked by the window unit and felt heat coming through its face of metal ribbons. The path curved back toward the main building, and the alley narrowed, and there was nothing at the end except for the door to his windowless room. He stood at the red metal door pulling out his keys, the stucco walls of the hotel surrounding him.

The unfinished pine wall was blond in the lamplight. He sat at the table cooling from his shower in a cotton bathrobe and looking at the pictures he had hung on the constellation of three nails left by some other tenant of another summer. He had stabbed the nail heads through the photo paper. Julie stood in the state park back home with a dark stripe of undyed roots down the center of her head. Her tank top left her freckled breastplate showing, and they were just friends now. He had hung a picture of a good friend. In the second picture, his family wore pastel clothes in front of an exploding white dogwood tree on Easter. The third, a black and white, had been taken before he was born. His grandfather, as a young man in law school, had sat slick-haired in a professional's studio.

His feet were tired. He stretched his arches on the red felt floor. Bricks as bookends held the few books he had brought with him, one brand new on fishing Caribbean waters, three novels, the Bible, an address book and a book of blank pages that he had written and drawn in.

He drew now in the blank book, weaving owls and human hands and pieces of architecture into one sprawling drawing. He leaned over the pages, pinning the book flat and concentrating. The television on the dresser behind him got its reception from coat hangers bent into rabbit ears, and balls of aluminum foil were formed around the ends. The screen showed a drama made fifteen years before, and the feather-haired actress performed false madness at her male co-star. Music swelled behind their voices and came out into the room through a panel of black holes that covered the speaker. It mixed with the Pan Dragon music leaking through the walls, and Kyle's pen came back across the page to one of the owls. He decided to draw a hat on top of its head between the ear tufts. He had seen a cartoon owl wearing a medieval yeoman's cap before, but he wanted to give his owl something different. He gave it a baseball cap, and he drew the calligraphic A of the Atlanta Braves logo on the front. Back home, he once drove down a narrow side street of the ghetto on his way home from an all night breakfast diner. Blond underwings came into his headlights. Kyle stopped, and an owl stood in the middle of the lane staring into the headlights of his running car. A cockroach crawled out from under the owl's talon and crawled disoriented on the asphalt. The owl looked down at the cockroach, and stepping with its talon, pinned the cockroach again. It leaned over and put its beak between its toes. The owl flew again, and the cockroach was eaten.

Kyle capped his pen and put it down on the table. He held up the drawing book looking at the whole picture, then closed it and put it back in line with the other books between the bricks. His terrycloth tie was loose. It fell off when he stood up, and his bathrobe hung open. He walked around the room with only himself underneath, pacing from the door to the bed to the dresser to the raw pane of mirror and then back to the bed. His alarm clock sat on the red felt floor beside the metal legs of the bed frame, and he moved it around with his foot. He bent down and set the alarm for seven in the morning. He wanted to get up early and see new parts of the island.

The Pan Dragon sounds died away. He opened the door to his room, and the alleys were quiet. He went back inside and knelt beside the mini-frig and took a small bucket of cookie dough ice cream out of the frost-covered freezer section. In the top drawer of his dresser, he had a cigarillo in its wrapper, a lighter and a box of plasticware. The assorted ends were down in the box, and he pulled out a knife and a fork before taking a whole handful out and finding a spoon by looking. He put the spoon and the cigarillo in his bathrobe pocket, and from the third drawer, he took a folded swimsuit that he had put away damp. He stepped into it, pointing his foot through the mesh lining and pulling it up, feeling the cold fabric on his thighs. He put his keys in the other pocket of his bathrobe, slid into his tennis shoes and walking on the folded down heels, went out into the night.

The door to the bathhouse was open. Steam roiled out, and light fell across the alley. He smelled the dank hot air, and through the metal slats covering the high bathhouse window, he heard shower water splattering on the tile floor, and someone's singing echoed in the stall. In the staff courtyard, the boy from Connecticut who worked in snorkel rentals played Midge's guitar, and a group was gathered around him listening. His eyes were closed tight. He sang and strummed the strings increasingly faster like some pleasure was reaching its peak, and Midge sat staring at his fretwork. They drank beer out of cans and bottles, and two girls in the gazebo slow danced with each other, out of time with the music. Kyle went by and didn't meet anybody. He came out on the beach and looked up at the two-tiered deck behind the main building of the hotel. Shapes of people, sitting and standing, broke up the lit panels of glass balcony doors, and the voices of people carried through the night air. There was still swimming in the pool, and bands of light scanned the stucco balconies. He heard the splash of a body, and the refracted beams shook on the hotel wall like projected images of microscopic creatures. He saw water spray up into the air like from the crater of a purified volcano, the glowing balls of water holding light from the old lampposts.

Dried palm fronds and bundles of bamboo hid the lumber and block foundation of the open-air beach bar. Blue and red neon coursed through curving tubes. The guitars were gritty and growling in the speakers, and Don and Maunar sat on stools at the bar. Don leaned forward with his pointed shoulder blades knifing through his undershirt, and she sucked on a black straw that led to a stemmed vase of thick white fluid. An arrangement of sliced produce clung to the rim. Down the bar, a group of thick young men stood swaying and drinking and bumping into each other. One took his frayed-billed hat off while he talked wide-eyed with sentiments. His head was shaved and burned pink, and he talked out over the music, poetic and rhythmic and coming back over and over to repeat a chorus whose great hook was a cuss word alliterated with "fantastic." People sat on the low seawall dangling their legs, and a group of combers pointed a flashlight into the water. They walked and darted the light looking for crabs. The beamed moved and showed dices of what happened. Their bucket and a pair of hibiscus-printed shorts. Then the sand and a foot with an aquasock. Children ran toward the beached catamarans. The masts lay in the sand underneath with the sails bundled around their poles. The children tried to jump on the canvas, and their father called out, "It's not a trampoline. Get down now please. Get down."

Kyle walked into the dark under the palms. He walked along by the bungalows and then the more modern condominiums whose stories curved with the crescent shape of beach. He avoided everyone, and he hoped no one saw him. The hemp hammock was empty. He took the cigarillo out of his pocket and unwrapped it. With the hard plastic filter between his front teeth, he leaned close to the leeward side of a palm trunk and turned the wheel of the lighter with his thumb. Yellow and blue sputtered and left, and he let go of the gas button. He tried it again inside the shield of his hand, and the wind knocked the flame down again and beat away its light. He turned himself and made use of his own body, and the flame jumped up straight, and the smell of the cigarillo was sweet. The smoke coated the inside of his mouth when he took it in, and a lightness hit his head. His stomach moved. He kept walking until he felt far away from everything. Then he sat down in the sand and smoked and stared at the dark water and listened to it.

The cigarillo was finished. He stood up, dusted sand from the seat of his bathrobe and ate the cookie dough ice cream. The cardboard bucket perspired in the night heat, and sand stuck to the moisture. He paced around eating, and it took the tobacco taste away and soothed his stomach. A limb snapped on the wooded slope, and the branches shook. The outer leaves shone and rocked in the penumbra hotel light, the marginal beach, and the darker leaves whispered behind them in the wind like actors backstage of a curtain. Then in the gap, he saw animal eyes glowing like signet rings. The head was invisible in the dark. Not a human composition, night disguised the face as nothing, and only eyes, hovering like little suns, stamped the night in mid-jungle, and he imagined what he must look like, recorded in a bathrobe by a basic mind. Seen by the unseen, anything could have happened to his image, transference into the psychedelic spectrums of a heat map, rotation, distortion, transparency. His form was in the wild thing. He put the plastic spoon into the ice cream again. The rocks of frozen cookie dough kept the core solid. He dug around the carton edges where the ice cream was softer and getting the spoon in was easier.

He walked up to the side of the condominium. Swimsuits dried on the rails, and an inflated killer whale float crowded the end balcony. The whale had kind blue eyes with piebald pupils and black plastic handles on its back. Past the rinse station with its overhead and knee-high nozzles of chrome, he went up the concrete steps flanked by white and pink oleanders. He crossed the end of the parking lot looking into the car windows and looking at license plates. Most were rental cars, bare of personality inside and out, and he climbed a set of sun-bleached wooden stairs up a bank covered on both sides by low-growing bushes and spindles of weed that shook erect in the wind and bowed when the gusts were over. He was close to the bottom of the ice cream bucket. Sluggish cream moved around and coated the one clump left frozen. Above the cul de sac of the dead-end road, a streetlight buzzed on its high pole putting a radioactive orange down on the weathered asphalt and the metal dumpster. Inside, he knew, were coconuts, removed to the metal mausoleum, and he went into the foliage, climbing a worn path of white sand. Dusty roots grew sideways across, terracing the path and making natural steps. Headlights from the road above came into the tops of the trees, highlighting specific branch and leaf segments and moving distorted shadows through the canopy of mimosas.

The path opened up to a weedy bank, and a metal guardrail sat on top at the roadside with yellow and black sharp-curve warnings sticking up on wooden posts. He saw a crushed Gatorade bottle and a littered lottery ticket. He picked up the ticket and read the instructions. The silver fields had been scratched off, and the player had played by the rules of the ticket and lost. The ticket wasn't worth anything. He threw it back down and stood looking at the trash with the empty ice cream bucket still in his hand. Cars came by on the road above, and he debated in his head for a long time before slinging his own trash against the bank. The plastic spoon fell out, and the cardboard bucket rolled down, barely heavy enough for gravity, until it hung on some plants and stayed as bright new litter, and he wondered how long it would take for it not to look out of place with the trash that had already been there for a long time.

He followed the road, keeping hidden below the bank and close to the trees. The well-lit canopy of the gas station across the road sheltered no business. A brown road sign pointed out a public beach to the right. He turned and went up the steep road heading toward the top of the mountain.

The parking lot at the top was empty. Another brown sign pointed toward an old cement archway and a staircase that curved down along the black, wooded slope of the mountain. A whitewash seemed to hold the arch together, keeping it from crumbling into a pile of feta. He stood on the landing looking down the staircase, and the sound of crashing waves bounced between the caracole walls. Wind blew into his hair and pushed it back off his head and gave him trichoesthesia. Chills and sensations fluttered down his spine and felt euphoric, and the wind was full of sticky salt that coated his body and filmed his eyes over with haze. He saw nebulas around the cardinal and white pegs of light that came from the other islands. He walked to the end of the parking lot on top of the mountain and stood on the last bumper, looking out at the Caribbean. Night in the water looked lonely. Far across were other continents and people living however they lived. He didn't know beyond stereotypes, and he could only guess using his imagination. All the notions and habits of others were facts of the world, and what was going on out there right then was becoming the history of the world. People were doing something, and then they had just done it, and it was history. But for the every day man, he thought, doing was as ephemeral as thinking in the course of everything. So the human kingdom was strange and unpredictable to him, and he knew he was too young to be wise. On the mountain at night wearing a bathrobe, he knew he looked like a pageant magi who belonged in a fellowship hall, but he also felt like a pilgrim of understanding. Going on top of lookouts had always made him imagine the world. His knowing was limited by the night and by his range of memories, and he was all the time looking for more experiences. Julie used to get undressed as ceremoniously as she had put clothes on. During thunderstorms, she liked to take off everything and stand on the quilted bed, facing the rain-beaten window pane. The lightning blued her nudity, and she screamed and applauded. Something fierce would be happening outside, but she was inside, stripped down to the soft and downy stuff of her that no one ever saw. He got to see it. He wondered if anyone got to now. God's flash bulbs, she called lightning, believing God made her but wanted to recapture her image. God was interested in her, and Kyle was interested in her. A different gust came strong at his bathrobe and lifted the flap and blew on his thighs. A passing boat put out a churn of wake in the liquid noir. Out of the black bathwater, the smear of stars. Scorpius crawled the wall of southern sky with claws extended in everlasting battle, the dying fall's birth sign, philosophical, domineering, willful, loyal. Her birthday was in the spring.

Coming back down, he followed the curving road looking for his ice cream bucket. He felt guilty for having littered the bank with it, and he wanted to pick it up and take it with him, but he never saw it again. He rounded a new curve and went up a bank he didn't remember from before. "Kyle. Kyle. Come over here." Don and Maunar saw him, and he didn't have a chance to hide. They waited for the dollar bus with other hotel employees who were just getting off, having cleaned and waited and bused the last tables. Don and Maunar wore their street clothes. A black gym bag sat on the pavement between them, holding their work uniforms, and children ran around playing, weaving through the adults and tagging each other and climbing up the poles of the bus stop shelter. They called his name, and he had to walk over to them in his bathrobe. "Hey Kyle."

"Kyle. Kyle. Come over here."

"Kyle."

"What's up?"

"Not much. What are yall up to?"

"We were about to leave hours ago, but Maunar wanted a drink in the bar before going home," Don said. "She lied though. She wanted three." He hugged her by the shoulders, and she pushed away and flicked her wrist to slap at his chest.

"Before going home to do what?" she said.

"Make me supper," Don said, winking at Kyle.

"No, no, to do what? Come on. You know the answer. Search deep behind your face for the answer," Maunar said. She looked at Kyle. "The answer is to take a bubble bath."

"She thinks she's going to take a bubble bath tonight," Don said.

"I am. I am going to take a bubble bath," she said.

"She's been thinking that since this morning," Kyle said. "She might really do it."

"I am. I am. Oh, I am." She put her arms in the air and turned in a circle.

"Come over. She'll make supper for you, too," Don said.

"Who says?"

"Oh no," Kyle said. "I'm fine. I just ate ice cream."

"Yeah, supper for us," Don said. "Ice cream isn't supper." He grabbed her chin and pulled her face close to his, squeezing her cheeks forward and puckering her lips artificially. He kissed them, and they looked like rubber, loose and unresponsive. "Just one supper for each of us." She slapped his wrist and moved back. "And you can make supper for yourself, too. Kyle and I don't mind. You can even sit at the table with us."

"Don't let him fool you. He wanted to have three drinks at the bar, too," she said. "It wasn't just me."

"We both wanted the drinks, had the drinks, and now it's suppertime. Kyle come with us?"

"Oh no. I'm not dressed or anything."

"Go get dressed. You have time."

"Yeah, cause I'm taking a long bubble bath first."

"It'll be a late supper. What time is it?"

"Late," Maunar said.

"So it'll be real late when we have supper. Who cares? You don't work tomorrow. Nobody works but me, and I don't care. We'll let her have her bubble bath. Give me a pen and something to write with."

"How about some paper, too?" Maunar said. She bent down to the gym bag and unzipped the end pocket. She brought out a pen and clicked the point in and out, and her billfold had a metallic gold heart set in the leather. She found a receipt inside. She read the print, "Shampoo and eggs. Okay, nothing embarrassing. You can write on the back of this. She stood up, and Don told her to lean over and make her back like a table. She put her hands on her knees and rolled her eyes and smacked her lips while he dug the point of the pen into the silky paper, wrinkling it to write. The directions were for the dollar bus and then where to go on foot after getting off. He handed them to Kyle. Kyle looked at them nodding, understanding. "I'll be there as soon as I go change and all," he said. He folded the receipt and put it in the pocket of his bathrobe.

The patty melts were gone. The plates sat greased from them still, shining under the low-hanging overhead, its wicker basket shade the broad shape of a ricer's hat. Cooler night air eased through the open window, and a box fan on a high stool in the corner battled the hot stove air and the bulb and people heat of the kitchen. The fan sang a droning song that kept its plastic blades spinning blurred, and the overhead lampshade swayed from side to side in the pushed air. Maunar sang with the song that came from the boom box on the kitchen counter. Her leg was in the chair with her, and she hugged it to her chest and picked at the grape bunch. Kyle watched her, and her tongue moved the smashed grapes around in her mouth. Shining slick with juices, the tongue formed the words of the song. She was a different race than he was, but the slick tongue still made the song. It was the same one she had been singing in the bathtub when he had gotten there.

He had stood in the den, and from down the dark hall, her voice had come from the rectangular corona of light, the door eclipsing song, singer, bathroom, bath and bather. Don had flipped the light on, and a milky ceramic bowl went on overhead, clinging to its firmament of mop-jabbed plaster, and the den was there. Dusty tea candles sat in a dish on top of a stack of blank CDs. A little iron whale pinned a pile of opened mail to the coffee table. Condensation ran down a yellow Wendy's cup, and a computer router sat overturned and disconnected under the ladder-back desk chair, one of its rubber-coated antennas disjointed at its swivel spot and showing guts of multicolored wire. A jar of blue-emu ointment sat on the armrest of the sofa.

"Sorry for the mess," Don had said.

"A maid lives here?"

"The cobbler's children run barefoot in the streets."

"Yeah, my dad used to teach piano. He was always too sick of giving lessons to work with me and my sister and make sure we practiced," Kyle had said.

Kyle looked at Maunar's leg above the tabletop, bent and bold in the low light of the overhead. He didn't know how long he had looked at her. The beer made him scared. He couldn't feel how his face looked or how long it stared, and he looked down at his lap. He wiped the neck of his beer bottle, then his mouth. Then he squeezed the paper towel into a tight ball and dropped it into his plate. It expanded and unwadded until the print of pastel ribbons and nosegays showed up again on the quilted surface.

"This song won't get out of my head," Maunar said.

"Because you play it over and over with the boom box," Don said. "If it's just in your head, we're telepathic because I hear it all the time, too." The cat jumped up in the empty fourth seat and sat with only its head above the tabletop like a child needing a booster seat. It climbed on the table and sat down, the possessed tail curling and lifting at the tip while the cat stared ahead.

"Hello, Amber," Maunar said. The body leaned forward, and the back end lifted. The mauve nose worked, and its cloven bangs of upper lip pumped under the black row of puncture holes where the filiform whisker needles made entry. Feeling invited, it sniffed the corkless neck of the chardonnay bottle and chewed its tatters of mangled black foil. Then it stretched to smell the grape bunch, exposing in its cream neck fur, patches of butterscotch and the dirty color of torched meringue. "No, Amber," Maunar said. She popped the cat's nose, and Amber recoiled, blinking and collapsing her neck so that her little fist of head sat on her chest again. A blackish navy chevroned a necklace, and Amber back-stepped over the salt and pepper shakers. The cat stretched down off the table, its body a strand of melting cheese falling into the chair seat and compacting again like the bellows of an accordion. She disappeared and showed up on the kitchen counter, cheeking the boom box antenna, and then on top of the baker's rack, she high-stepped through the knickknacks it held, a black angel statue with prismatic robe, a white teddy bear wearing a red bowtie, the tag still in its ear like a cardboard piercing, a bamboo backscratcher, an unopened bottle of Coke commemorating the 1996 Olympics in Atlanta. Stepping over to the refrigerator, the cat huddled down and stretched its dusty arms, letting them hang over the top edge of the freezer door.

"She likes it up there. I guess it's warm," Don said.

"Did yall go to the Olympics?" Kyle said looking at the baker's rack.

"I have a sister that lives in Atlanta. She sent us that bottle, not until 1998, though."

"I went to the Olympics. I went to see football, but it was really soccer."

"Was it fun?"

"Yeah, I had a good time."

"Let me find the keyboard," Don said, standing up. "Kyle knows how to play."

"Find the screwdriver so you can fix the frying pan handle, too," Maunar said.

He moved his patty melt plate, and Don put the keyboard down in front of him and put two drums of D battery in his hand. Kyle flipped the keyboard over and opened the door. Two old batteries lay inside, and bluish-white corrosion, like crusted toothpaste, clung to the nodes. He took them out and blew on the coils and laid the new batteries in the half-cylinder compartment. The springs pushed them tight against each other. Flipping the keyboard back over, the power bulb lit up red when he clicked the bar over, and it was live. The plastic key he tested had no weight, and he used the trumpet setting and turned a beat on, adding more percussion by pressing orange octagonal buttons. It sounded like the soundtrack for a karate movie, the effects for punches, a batch of beaten celery. He moved his right hand across the keyboard like a newborn spider learning to walk. The bottom of the frying pan was burned and stained with grease in Don's hand. He twisted the screwdriver and tightened the pan's handle.

"Stop playing around and play a real piece," Don said.

"It's not a real piano. I think I'm using it how you're supposed to."

"Did you fix it?" Maunar said.

"It's tighter."

"Let me see," she said, reaching for the frying pan. She held it by the handle and mock sautéed with it. "It's better," she said. "Thank you."

"Play a Bach song," Don said.

"I'm telling you, I didn't get very far."

"Well bring it out back and play a lullaby or something for me to howl at the moon by."

On the central mountain of the island, the green clapboard was built into the rise of hinterland, so from the gravel drive, the roof covered a squat story that didn't look to shelter all it held, a quadruplex, four different households in one structure. On the cross of vine-hosting posts out front, different letter stickers stuck to the four mailboxes. On the back deck, the house dropped with the hillside and became a tower of three floors, a pergola for clinging vegetation. Decks and lattice. The neighbor below was out. She looked up from her landing with a segment of green amaryllis stem in her mouth. She inhaled through the tube and exhaled nothing into the night. "I know this is strange," she said, "but I can't afford a nicotine inhaler."

Kyle restarted the keyboard beats. The neighbor sang and made up a song and pretended to smoke the amaryllis stem. Hookless and free form and diverse in content, the lyrics ranged from folk philosophy to a description of her rapport with a grocery store employee. "We thanked each other face to face once. We've smiled in the aisles, but we never once hung out," she sang, and Kyle used aqua arrows to increase the tempo and keep up with her, the poet of the island hilltop, reverberating from her sinuses and boiling new combinations of everyday speech. The song came catchy and left ephemeral, not ever returning or making sense again or following up on a single phrase of melody or idea of verse, like spitting ticker tape fed into a trashcan fire, and the news of the current mind was a forgotten file compared to the most recent updates. Kyle played along with chords and notes, so the keyboard rocked on the swagged surface of the weathered deck rail. Don shuffled his feet across the floorboards, dancing. His worn hightop soles whispered on the wood. His beer foamed high in the neck of his bottle and ran down his hand to patter beside the footwork. The footwork stomped the foam and spread it into the boards to wet them dark, and the moon had already set. Sweat cried from his brow. He was quiet, but his face turned up over the roof toward the red beacon of the mountaintop radio tower. His lips pursed in pantomime howl. Slow red pulses showed the surrounding framework in each blink, and in the background, the city lights of Charlotte Amalie faded a light patch in the shell of black sky. Spinning, the other way, downhill, an ocean liner moved on the water like a harmonica lit from within, veering slowly from its rhumb line to join the channel traffic, and in every vessel, vehicle or man, a song was visible through the reedy windows, and at the horizon, lightning crawled through lanterns of cloud. Maunar came out with another juice glass full of white wine, and they were at it and in full throes. She watched her husband's face, and it was transformed with the ecstasy of dance. His body was only a designation in a large expanse, and he seemed on the brink of spastic levitation. His face was blank and loose, whipped by his moves and unattractive. He was more than just the form she saw. He had shaken free of himself and was gone from controlling his body entirely, and so was Kyle and so was the neighbor who chanted from her porch below, and they were gone somewhere, each to his own place by way of his own instrument, body, voice, Casio keyboard.

The scene proceeded with the storm cloud sweeping by the island, and the great zeppelin of cloud, violent within and bruised by an air on purple fire, issued down concentrated tendrils of corded lightning that dragged the surface of the water, stinging and sizzling it to an instant boil, and its hanging haul was a dark drape of rain that blotted out the lights of the harbor town across the channel during its passing. Both islands, skirted by only the storm margins and mists, missed the percussive core of downpour. Only the smell of rain floated up the mountainside as a new humidity, and the evaporated pocket of sky water filled the cavities of their faces with fresh issue, and they returned to themselves. They returned slowly. They rewound to a more normal time and rebottled the spirits of themselves that had been jangling wild at the ends of stretched tethers like hundreds of kites bobbing in the sky above the house. They came back into their eyes, looking around, looking up and looking at each other. It was just the mechanical keyboard beat that didn't quit the trance, and its trance was flawless. It beat steady. It beat perfect, deadpan, steady.

He woke up looking across a plain of yellow pillow. The weight of his head sank and creased the case so a starburst of little gullies led from his face, and the corner of his open mouth rested against the thin fabric, breathing in cool dry air that came from the window unit above his head. He closed his mouth, and it was waxed and coated. The window unit cycled off, and the compressor shuttered to die. The quiet sounds of the house took the place of the air conditioner noise, and the last of the air sank down on his body under the sheets. He moved his leg. A ticking clock crescendoed in the new quiet, and the prevalence of sound was reordered. The clock noise came from the kitchen, and he sat up in a sofa bed that pulled out into their living room. The curved gray screen of the television set showed Kyle his fun house reflection. His hair stuck up in loops at the crown. He touched them, and the spring-loaded curls rebounded to resist order on his head. Curtains were pulled against the blast of light out. Someone froze time during the pinnacle of a great explosion, and that was the tropical day. The coffee table, pulled to the side, made room for the collapsing bed, and going to sleep was coming back to him. The coffee table reminded him of the preparations. He scooted across the mattress, the mechanisms of the pullout creaking. He swung his legs over the edge, and the metal elbows of the bed's workings dug into the backs of his knees. The bars and hinges looked like parts of an animal trap. He had slept in his gray cutoffs. Standing up, bars of sunlight from the curtain gaps angled across the surfaces of the room, and shining motes winked through the fields above the rays, showing the shadowed room what a jazzed zone could do to just dust. The dust was pretty. Walking, a bar of light came across his eye. He looked toward the curtain gap, and his whole head filled with a great white flash. It blinded him. He turned away with his eyes closed, and white's negative, every color, bloomed on the backs of his eyelids.

Embarrassment came from nowhere, and he remembered knocking the keyboard off the deck rail. He had looked down at it where it landed on the neighbor's deck below. Batteries rolled across the unprocessed planks. "Kyle, I think you'd better stay here tonight," Maunar had said.

"If we're going to start a band, all we need is a lead guitar, bass, drummer and a singer."

"And a keyboardist," he remembered saying.

"And a keyboard, now."

Beads hung between kitchen and den. Blond and dark wooden balls arranged by stain made geometries down the strings. Like drops of a weak waterfall frozen in midair, the beads hung still and portioned. He used the backs of his fingers to part them and go through, easing his hands together behind his back, supporting the beads so they wouldn't collide and tap. He looked for the clock that ticked. He found a black oval framed by brass. The gold second hand jerked over the numerals and the dashes between. Almost noon and no sounds came from the back of the house. The window was closed now, and the sheet rock walls of the kitchen shut off the sensory effects of the living day. The blades in the box fan stood visible with stillness and furry with clinging dust. On the table, a mangled shape of yellow legal paper curled where the strip was ripped unclean, and Maunar's deliberate letters sat fat and squat in red ink on the page. He was the only person in the house.

At the sink, he lifted the stainless steel arm and twisted it to the right for cool water. He put his head in the basin. Falling water stirred the air in the metal tub and dredged the smell of old dishwater through the rubber epiglottis of the drain's flaps. He drank and concentrated on taking long slow breaths through his nose. Standing up again, the water ran down his chin in a cool line over his knot of larynx. He wiped it away and watched the water flowing out of the faucet. He put his head into the sink again. Out of the corner of his eye, he saw the water circling the drain in a holding pattern, swirling calyxical on its way down. He stood up, and his stomach felt full of water, and the green digital clock on the microwave said the same thing the real clock had said. He didn't have anywhere to be, and the green numbers in the dark under the cabinets didn't really matter.

Outside, he took his shirt off and stuffed as much of it as he could into his back pocket. He walked up the gravel drive, and the sun came into his skin. He was already dark from having lived on the island three weeks, and his skin was the color of a deer or a brown paper bag. He hadn't had a haircut since late winter. His hair was starting to curl, and he could see blurry sweeps out of the corners of his eyes. The curls were turning copper and shining like high-end pipes. He squinted in the daylight. On the narrow street, he walked along the rocks and high grass of the shoulder, looking for the bus stop. The small yards were crowded with broad-leaf bushes and jungle plants, and some of the plants looked dangerous like pointed daggers spiraling out of squat pods. He passed intricate blossoms, lobed like hearts and held stabbed by their tall green stems. Swollen pouches hung like saddlebags, beckoning and ripe like they could burst at anytime and invert into juicy folds. A woman on a porch threw her hand up to him, and he threw his hand up. Cars crawled by, and he moved into the yards for them to pass. He took a left and walked downhill through another neighborhood of loud colored houses, each front door facing a different direction without regard for the street. Heat came off the pavement. He didn't have socks, and his feet slid forward in his hot shoes, and the shirt hanging out of his back pocket brushed the backs of his legs. In the shade of a striped awning, a cat was on top of another cat next to an empty Gatorade bottle, and the one on the bottom moaned with a cry that almost sounded human. A breeze felt good blowing through his chest hair and stomach hair. The endorphins from movement were hitting him in the brain. He felt goodness radiating up through the core of his head and spreading out to his temples, and he felt his pulse in his fingertips. He didn't care about not finding the bus stop and being lost.

He saw two young boys in a yard ahead. The younger wore cartoon print underroos, and they took turns using a bike that was too big for both of them. They stood on a crate to mount the seat and stalled to fall on purpose against a weed-covered bank when the other yelled to switch. They stared at him passing and said something he didn't understand. He nodded and looked down at the street. The grit sparkled, and he didn't look up again until he passed them. He didn't know how long he had walked. The sun beat down and warmed his hair. He felt his hot crown with the palm of his hand and wound through the clustered houses, the crooked lanes weaving through one neighborhood after another. Then the street became more of a road. It curved into shade where his perspiration worked better, and he put his shirt back on and adjusted the collar. The houses stopped in favor of tall trees to the right that were dressed by thick hanging vines, and they looked like monsters being born of the growth. To the left, open space and a drop off. He crossed the road and walked to the edge and didn't see anything that looked familiar to him in the green and the rooftops and roads below. It was a different view than he had seen before, a part of the island he didn't recognize, new water and the shape of a new span of coastline, map-like in the distance, and stand-alone islands of rock rose humpbacked and ancient out of the blue. He kicked gravel over the edge, and the rocks fell down through the bare sticks that grew crooked out of the dusty wall of cliff. He crossed back through the patchy shade to the deeper shade and came up on a cluster of cars and mopeds parked in a narrow crescent of gravel on the shoulder. People stood around a teardrop trailer that sat hitched to nothing. White smoke slipped from an arm of pipe that hailed from the end window, and Kyle came into a zone where the smell of grease mixed with the wet breath of plants. His stomach responded instantly. He felt it constricting and tugging at his esophagus so that he tasted his own spit, and the ridged roof of his mouth itched, and he was hungry.

He stood in line staring at the neck of an old black man in front of him. Cables that ran up to tether the cranium showed under his tight skin, and the man wore a plaid shirt of blue, pink, green and purple stripes that intersected on a faded field of black background, the threads worn so the elements shone and blew through, and his tight little trunk stood silhouetted inside like a column of antique muscle that looked to have supported hard work for a long time. His slack formless collar slinked loose down his back, exposing the first few knots of his spine. Kyle cocked his hip to look around a foam hat that sat high on the man's pile of hair, and the menu items were written on a poster board in streaky marker. The Feast of Beast sandwich Kyle ordered was an envelope of pressed bread holding sliced hotdog, jerk goat and seasoned whitefish dressed with mustard and mayonnaise and onions and peppers. Kyle brought from his back pocket, the canvas wallet that his body had given a gluteus curve, and he paid for the sandwich and a Coke that came in a glass bottle. The young girl inside the trailer stretched her gum into big pink bubbles that gyrated in the push of the plastic mini-fan clipped on the window frame. She unwrapped his paper straw for him and forced it down the throat of the bottle. Foam inside attached itself to the tube, and the gas lifted the straw until it wedged in the curved neck, most of it leaning out the mouth at a low angle, and the food came up immediately, wrapped in wax paper and passed to granddaughter from grandmother who hovered above two paraffin stoves, cooking and portioning in the dark umbra of caboose kitchen, her working head a primitive bullet in the felt cloche hat she wore, its sweat-stained ribbon tightly knotted to cinch a wavy rim above her brow. The granddaughter slid the sandwich to Kyle. He cradled it in the arm that held his Coke and with the other hand took squares of paper towels that she passed to him.

In the carport of flora, the people ate lunch, sitting on benches, some standing around a card table, others eating off the dull, sun-washed hood of a Fiero. The radio inside played through the open windows, news and then the weather and then the jingle of the station. A quartet sang the call sign. Warped noises and breakbeat sound effects attacked like extraterrestrial weaponry before the disc jockey came on speaking through his buttered fauces about the midday heat. He was somewhere out of the studio, beachside, under a tent giving away T-shirts. He talked about the adrenaline-fueled scene and the excitement, but a sluggish undertone of summer laziness lay embedded in his narration, like the words hummed deadpan in his head, but by professional rote, the equipment of his speech released ornamental inflection. He said a beach volleyball game was just starting up.

Kyle listened to the radio and watched the people. He sat on the ground in the dust and sparse gravel, eating his sandwich away from everyone. His forearms propped on his bent legs were lunch-rigged limbs, and he rocked forward into the sandwich, eating fast and getting messy and not minding, not knowing anyone. A wan mayo and mustard mixture smeared the side of his hand, and the Coke was quick to turn warm, burning his tongue and the back of his throat. The paper straw stuck to his dry lips, and he licked them with his Coke-coated tongue and darted his eyes back and forth from his sandwich to the people, from the curved shapes his mouth dragged out of the pressed bread, to the Saturday laborers on their noon breaks. Two little girls came running, and a wife came after, wheeling her hips down the road to meet one of the men and eat with him. The girls finished their food fast to do a jump rope act for him, and the father sat watching the girls, grinning toothy, listening to the accompanying kiddy chant and watching the ground get beaten up into a dust cloud around them. Kyle watched, too, and planned his bites and made sure to savor the thick middle. Biting again, pillows of sliced hot dog fell condiment-covered out the back of the sandwich, and riding the case edges like runaway wheels, they circled before settling flat, coated by dust on the ground in front of him.

The empty wax papers started disappearing, consumed by the fists of the men. They pitched their wads at metal drum beside the trailer and laughed at those who missed, and they sat or leaned against something, palming their mouths and wiping their necks and pumping their hats on and off their heads. The Fiero's mid-engine sang in a high idle like a sewing machine under the trees until the driver put it in gear and dropped the tone. The driver turned backwards, embracing the passenger-side headrest to look through the rear glass and steer the Fiero into the road in reverse. The ones on foot milled casually toward a path that went into the woods, and the group thinned and started single-file into the dark tunnel of vegetation. A straggler kept looking at Kyle, a young man in a long white button up shirt, his sleeves rolled in tight cuffs above his elbows.

"Hey," he said.

Kyle kept quiet.

"Hey, man," he said. He left the others in their pack swaying towards the woods. He came over to Kyle who still sat on the ground. The man crouched beside him, cockeyed with sclera the color of a low gold moon and a knotted, asymmetrical face. "Do you have a computer?"

"There's a computer at work," Kyle said.

"Can you look up these Dragon Ball figures for me?" He passed Kyle a folded piece of paper with pretty writing in a scrolling hand of thick black ink, and it listed foreign-sounding names in three perfectly straight lines like some colonial document intended for a ceremonial reading.

"You mean on eBay or something?"

"To see how much they're worth."

"I can't really use the work computers for anything like that," Kyle said. "So I don't think I could look them up. They won't let me use the computer for that."

"Do you know how much they're worth?"

"No, I don't know anything about those," Kyle said.

"I can't get to the library, but they have a computer there," the man said.

"You might could look it up in some kind of magazine. There might be a trade magazine for that sort of thing."

"Where is that?"

"I don't know, maybe even the grocery store. I'm not really sure, though."

"The grocery store?"

"Maybe," Kyle said, and the man held out his hand asking for the list back. Kyle gave it to him, and the man reread the names, squinting at the paper and moving his lips.

"I have these figures. Do you think they're worth a lot?" he said.

"I have no way of knowing," Kyle said.

"Alright then."

"Sorry," Kyle said.

"Alright then," the man said, and he stood up, put the paper in his breast pocket and ran into the woods, catching up with the others.

Following them at a distance, the sun spots rode over their shirts. Ahead on the beaten sandy path, they walked through a hall of woods where beams of golden light fell through gaps in the ceiling like support beams in a mystical architecture of the future where transparencies could be tangible and wavelengths could be altered for use as building materials, and grown ups could sit on the invisible and laugh holding nothing like they do when they hold a glass they've emptied, and he also pretended to be in the ancient past walking with a pack of early men. He envied those who did get to live at the reckoning of time, but he didn't know whether he could survive prehistory's therapy of brutality. Violent urges still came standard with the package of man, he thought. A little dog came from somewhere. It passed Kyle on the path and ran to catch up with the line of men. It stopped to scratch, kicking itself in the head, getting up and running on. The sandwich had tasted good. It was heavy inside him. He walked slow not to catch up with the men, but he followed them and listened to their voices mix in with bird calls and bleating beetles who hid the violin strings of their wings under all the leaf hands hanging ever-ready for high fives, like ornaments on the pathside bushes, and he thought he heard the sound of the plants being alive, and it sounded like his own life, the one he heard when he covered his ears and held his breath. The difference between black and dark green. The difference between white and green. The difference between glossy and leathery, and the difference between fleshy and furry, the woods organized its members, putting the tough-skinned plants at the top to shield the kingdom of soft tissue inside, and he followed the men to a chain-linked fence that ran through the woods, and they stooped through a hole cut in the diamonds. The men kept walking. Kyle stopped at the fence hole, hung his hand on the links by his hooked fingers and looked after the men he had had lunch near. They descended the path into the sun toward some sort of factory with its own water tower. Working smoke stacks aimed out of the center building like cannons locked on their zenith.

Kyle left the path and climbed up through the bushes that grew out of the bank like antlers. He touched the wooden trunks that supported the setup and braced himself on them to climb through the thicket, along the path and then uphill again, off the path. A dark section of tree had fallen out of the canopy. It hung suspended in the house of growth by a network of vines that seemed to have gone after the timber in freefall, holding it caught, neither growing limb nor grounded log, and he pushed underneath it through the low plants that held onto his waist. He came into a tough, spiny population that shot up above his head with orange sexuality, and the traffic in the air was made of attracted bugs who buzzed veined petals of wing skin to approach the loose tongues of the corollas, and they landed to stuff themselves headlong into the flower holes. The habits of the plants were aggressive, and the plants were slutty, looking good in a cheap, high-wattage way but lacking the brilliance of the slow-growing hardwoods farther down the mountain. These erupted from the ground without care, and they weren't ashamed to grow with a young man there watching. They cascaded with the slope in the heavy humidity.

On a ridge, Kyle looked down into a small bowl of open land that hung at the hip of the mountain, and a crop grew there, fluorescent green in the sun. Men on the opposite rim of the bowl sat in banded lawn chairs, smoking in the shade, and Kyle smelled grass and saw a long rifle hanging by its strap from a knotted limb. He was close enough to read what the puff-paint on the man's shirt said, and the grinning one had bright teeth under the curling black hair of his mustache. They didn't see him or know he was there. They talked, and Kyle hid in the middle of thick plants. He watched his steps and paid attention to the ground underneath his tennis shoes, walking away from the weed bowl, stooped and cautious and getting out of there.

Farther up the hill, the bower for a nap, he thought, climbing into it. Inside, the thick was a pretty pitch, and the twisted boughs of an old tree stretched out in all directions like the purple energy bands of plasma spheres sold at the mall. The limbs held a dome of space out of the foliage, and he dropped to his knees on a bed of soft green covering whose tiny leaves folded with his touch. He put his head down, and the greenery came to eye-level so he saw the tiny leaves reopening like dozens of scrolls in his face, and he hooked his arm to hang his finger down and touch them again and watch the show. The sandwich slowed him down, and sleep welled up in him, metabolizing lunch and all he had seen and who he was on the island, and the inland fugue within a fugue was dissociative for his identity. His body took on the relaxed speed of the plants. He played with them and got lazy, and his thoughts went out and everywhere, and he was excited to be lying there, and he had had supper with actual residents the night before, and he was seeing everything and feeling like he was really living there for the first time, picking up stories to take back home with him after the summer was over and trying to remember them and have nostalgia for the present. Arched arboreal buttresses, he looked up into the cathedral of trees surrounded by biology, and he felt biological himself like he could be right there blinking and living and that was all there was to being alive, and anything holy in the world was an imitation of what he saw and felt. He kept blinking and breathing. He looked up into the trees who stood like giant monks, always vowing silence, and the sky was a cap of gold foil covering the treetops like leftovers. The spangled field of splintered heaven closed his eyes for him, and he didn't feel anything. Spots of light and gray moved in the hole like the translucent hide of a spiritual leopard, and the sun got his face and warmed it and influenced his dreams and made them wild. The drug of sun could change every perception, he thought, and the drug of sun flipped him out inside, and his body responded by itself, rolling him over so his nose hit the shy stuff, furling it again, and his eyelid spasmed with the eyeball rolling back and forth underneath it. He fussed and gripped the air in his sleep like a toddler ape until the spot moved on and his mind cycled again in the shade. He rolled over on his back, his abdomen ballooning with huge slow breaths of contentment. He turned over on his other side and pulled his knees up close. He felt cozy and delicate in his subconscious thoughts, like he had crawled up the soft neck of mother nature and become unborn again in the curls that weren't long enough to fit in her ponytail.

"Honey." He came to, crawling and holding his puffed lips loose. "Honey." It came from across the bower sounding like a voice, and he crawled across and up the bank to its edge and fell onto his chest, looking through the wall of leaves at a little field of yard with high grass and a white two-story whose paint peeled in big sections like newspaper pages. The house was backed into the woods on the other side of a narrow dirt driveway, and the vines pulled at the boards trying to drag them in. Slaw, the one with the puff-paint shirt, sat gonging his feet into the tin sheet that skirted the bottom of the porch, and the rhythm he kicked went with the music coming from inside, a powerful bass beat, and the windows of the house were raised halfway like doped eyes. Diamondy, the one with the mustache, stood in the yard by the porch, cane-leaning on the rifle and covering the barrel hole with his palm. The gun butt pivoted in the dirt, and a rooster on the corner of the porch jerked its head back and forth, jostling its gauntlet of iridescence neck feathers, trying to get both of its eyes on everything there was to see. A whole row of men sat slapping at each other on a vinyl porch couch without legs, and a ten-year-old Bronco inched up the steep driveway. Parking in the yard, its door panels forest green at the top, faded down to silver at the running board like sunset on an alien planet. The door opened. The driver got out wearing an oversized black shirt with a man's face screen-printed in metallic gold, and his sunglasses covered his eyes under the brim of a floppy white sailor's hat. "Honey." Kyle jerked his head over. The voice came from somewhere closer than the house, but he didn't see anyone. "Honey." The voice had started in his dreams. Its source was still unclear. He was still waking up and trying to rev himself out of the crazed feeling of fitful napping and into an understanding of the situation. "Honey." It came staccato and maybe from a different direction every time, like an audio effect of surround sound and hard to track. The men by the house looked and talked and shrugged, not knowing, too, and then they turned over their shoulders and called across the yard. They each took a turn calling, and they called the same name with cupped hands at their mouths. Toward Kyle, they called a name.

A man stood up out of the waist-high grass. They called him Zataurus. His black back naked in the sun, the lion tattoo between his shoulder blades inked out a forward pounce. The colors were dulled by such black skin, visible but not popping, like a phantom highlighter sketch drawn on carbon paper. He held his arms out toward the house in disbelief, rippling trapezius and deltoid. Bending down again in the grass, he picked up a jacket and put it on over just his skin to complete the fitted white suit, and close enough to be heard in a stage whisper, with only a thousand stalks of still grass between them, Kyle lay on his stomach watching. Zataurus moved through the grass toward the house.

"Honey."

"She can't hear you. The music is too loud."

Upstairs above the porch roof, a face came into the window out of the lampless room and into the same intensity of brightness that excited the white of the house. "I can hear you. I'm coming," she said in a soft, unnatural yell that rode the beats, and a curtain of blond waves wagged across the opening in a blast of isolated gold movement. Zataurus's white suit in the sunlit grass was too much for eyes that had been closed in the shade, and throwing so much of the light back, the white crept off the suit and into a halo that glided along with him and bled over to superimpose a blur on the tasseled mob of stalks and chevroned fibers of the top heavy grass. She appeared leaning against the front door jamb in her hot pink bikini bottoms, and Zataurus nodded and made finger circles out by his side. She nodded and walked forward onto the porch, her nipples like pink morsels of gum leading and parting the spaniel waves of hair that hung down her chest. The men on the low porch couch suppressed their jangling faces, and each looked in a different direction to subdue themselves. Her black top hung drying on a line that stretched between the porch posts, and she put the fingers of her hands in the cups to lift the top off. Ties trailing, she went back into the house, and Zataurus pumped his fist in the air. Everyone piled into the Bronco, Honey coming out last, unrushed and walking slow and perfect in the melting heat, her swimsuit covered by a muumuu printed with giraffes, elephants, myna birds and caladiums. They rode off down the driveway with the back glass open. Dusty high tops and thin black ankles stuck out the back, propped on the hatch and rocking with the bumps the truck hit on the road.

In their wake, Kyle walked out of the bushes and into the scene where a new protocol of quiet vacancy settled over the grass and the stolid house with unblinking windows and a stoic brow of shingles. The sun was burning him again and covering him in a thickness, so his blood was a reduction and any thoughts vaporized in the flow of molasses light that poured over him, slowing him, and he looked to see if the sun had gotten bigger. It sat staring out of the sky, a prominent force, impossible to face, but he tried again, and that was his exercise. The big fruit on fire. His eyeballs caramelized, and his eyes watered in the swirling overload of exposure. A green and brown blackout of burnout pulsed on top of everything he tried to look around seeing, and his tear water was filled with nectarized light. He was happy and staggering and spinning in the field looking up and down, and he couldn't believe life, and he thought he was stupid for grinning so big by himself, but he didn't feel alone either, doing swollen-headed stumblings, drenched in long draining ropes of viscous rays. His shimmering eyes saw with more importance because they were stained with light, and he promised himself he would always make time to kill. Like this, the kind of thing that happens, he thought, and it felt like the entire sun was inside his head where his life used to be.

The ghost man hung around on the terrace. He was the ghost of Blackbeard, and spotted tile ran out in a harlequin pattern to the rail where coin-operated viewfinders stood like little sentinels guarding the vista. The view was down the mountain to Charlotte Amalie. An overhanging terrace cantilevered over the sloped garden. Fathers pulled around the circular drive letting clean, sun-red families out for early suppers, and Blackbeard's Tower looked like a mound of sand dumped from a giant child's toy bucket. An empty pool still rocked from afternoon use. Chlorine was airborne. Kyle smelled the musty chemicals and neared a long dark corridor that led toward the restaurant. The sun fell into the mouth of the gallery but didn't reach far inside, and old lanterns took over, hanging in the arched ceilings, the curling flames fed by gas and reflected in the panes of the glass boxes. Display cases lined the wall to the left, and show lights lit old pirate relics, engraved swords, a mahogany chest with worn leather straps, silver hairbrushes, bracelets, ivory-handled magnifying glasses and brass napkin holders.

He walked up to the hostess podium. She wore a man's black necktie, the end tucked into her apron. She led him into the dining room through a door guarded by large chess pieces, and she sat him at a table at the end of the restaurant where the view was all encompassing. A server came with a pewter pitcher frosted and filled with ice water. Kyle pulled his linen napkin out of his drinking glass, shook out its fancy folds and laid it across his lap. The waiter filled the glass with ice water. Kyle drank all of it, and the ice moved forward and hit him in the upper lip. He put the glass back down on the tablecloth and wiped his mouth with the linen napkin, smelling its detergent. He tried to catch his breath without gasping and making noises, and he looked for the waiter to come back with the frosted pitcher. The roots of the trees in the garden grew curling down the hill like tangled octopus legs, and the waiter came back with the frosted pitcher and a wicker basket that he put down on the table. He refilled Kyle's glass. Kyle drank all of the water until there was just ice left. He unfolded the black napkin covering the top of the basket, and a pile of golden rolls filled the inside. He took one out, and it was hot. He put it down on his bread plate. Pats of butter wrapped in foil sat arranged fanwise in a saucer, and he took one and unwrapped it. He pinched a piece of bread, knifed a corner from the butter pat and stuck it into the soft pillow of roll. He held his glass up to his mouth and shook ice out and sucked on a piece until it melted. The menu came, and Kyle unfolded the sections looking for oysters on the half shell. They were too expensive. Everything on the menu was too expensive or market price, and Kyle stood up and walked over to the bar.

A man took away two glasses of white wine. Kyle liked the way the wine looked and asked the bartender what it was. The bartender, a squat little man wearing a black vest and bowtie, said three titles Kyle didn't recognize. The foreign language sounded like a pigeon's coo, and Kyle asked for a glass of house white wine. The bartender brought the bottle up from behind the bar, cradled it in a white towel and presented the label. Kyle didn't look at it. He looked down at his lap and said the wine was fine. The bartender poured it and put his glass in front of him on a cocktail napkin. Kyle drank it fast like he had the water, and then he left the restaurant.

At sea level again in Charlotte Amalie, he sat on the bench waiting for the dollar bus and looking down at a melted creamcicle on the sidewalk. The birch stick was coated and nearly buoyant in the cream, and the cruise ship was a monument in the harbor, towering above the shops behind him and blasting its discordant horns, asking the passengers to come back out of the town and reboard. Storefronts lined the street with rambling displays behind their picture windows. There were airbrush artists, braiders, taffy makers, glass blowers, whirligig dealers and screen-printers. The traffic, on the wrong side of the street, like in England, was almost stopped. People crossed in front of the cars, and they were loaded down with wide, glossy shopping bags. Kyle saw the top of the dollar bus way back in the jam. He stood up and walked in a circle around the bench he had been sitting on. He kicked the birch stick out of the cream pool, and he looked down at the cut across his palm. It had just started hurting, and he had just noticed it. From one of the thorn bushes, he thought. He heard a different language, and two boys who looked Swedish talked and laughed coming out of a store. Their white hair had been plaited and beaded, and they wore tie-dyed pants made out of loose jersey cotton. They had just bought the pants, and they helped each other pull the tags out of their elastic waistbands.

Harbor water bathed in the late slanted sunlight. The wave troughs were shadowed, and the low crest faces rode dim, their backsides golden, and the surface grew a darkness like a glass chimney collecting soot. Kyle stood on the diving platform. A strip of black electrical tape stuck to his shimmering green swimsuit. He ran his fingers across the piece, pressing down. Then he jumped into the water and followed thick-linked chains coming off each corner of the platform to a hoop of truck wheels and a washtub filled with rocks. He swam underwater toward clusters of coral reef, and the curls stretched out of his hair, and he saw the copper strands in the water, floating away from his head between his underwater strokes.

The reefs sat on the sandy bottom stacked like dishes in the bottom of a sink. The velveteen formations grew in autumns colors, and there were billowing structures like burned clouds and clouds on fire. Swaying parts like slices of iridescent roast beef wagged in the flow, and Kyle swam through long underwater tendrils of algae and plants like blades of peacock feathers and yards of unspooled thread extending through the water. Projections of membrane brushed his arms and effleuraged his sides and love handles and legs, and ivory bushes twisted up like distorted candelabra from the heaps of porous bone and hulled brain and tub sponge. He dove down farther. He blew air bubbles from his mouth trying to sink, and a rusted neocortex nestled in the fire coral. Fish of all sorts darted in and out of the holes and hid behind the corrugated shapes and structures, furry balloons and muffins with manes. Fish had knotted heads. Trumpet lips kissed the liquid, and tiger-striped and mushroom-fleshed fish swam with svelte velvet-faced angels. Rays hang-glided through canopies of malt spilled still in the water. Purple nodes and pincushion creatures stuck with aqua needles clung to formations like wadded up parachutes. A clown fish chased a clown fish, and a long swimming lizard with phosphorescent racing stripes did a flip and crawled through the water, parting a school of sideways kites trailing ribbons fringed with cirri. The reef was a biological bazaar where the life bartered gases, bubbles and particles, and teeming things gave a final show of energy before the end of day. It was the situation imitated by aquariums. His chest felt tight. He went up. Bobbing with his head above the surface, he breathed. He took his goggles off, rinsed away the condensation and rubbed his eyes.

He saw a sea turtle. He followed it, trying to get close, and it teased him, going buoyant and diving down again and keeping just ahead of him, leading him away from the reefs, across the harbor. He stayed near the surface, looking down at the sea turtle who skimmed along the sandy bottom. When the turtle came up for air, it flipped hard, rocking the shield of shell to get ahead of Kyle and keep its distance. It stuck its beak through the surface, and its round nostril holes gaped in the air. Kyle was close enough to see a gray ring around its eye. Kyle reached out to it, and he saw his hand magnified in front of him by the water, and he was shocked. His hand wasn't even that close to the sea turtle, not as close as he thought it would be. The water had tricked him, and he kept swimming. The sea turtle went back down again. It swam under the hotel's diving platform and stirred up a cloud in the settled sand near the makeshift anchors. It swam toward the submerged rocks at the edge of the harbor and blended in with them, swimming with a peaceful rhythm and swiveling with the crags to keep its blond plastron low to the angled surfaces. Kyle looked up and saw how close they had gotten to the mangrove limbs that rooted in the shallows and hovered off the hill slope above the water.

The turtle headed out toward the mouth of the harbor. The rocks got bigger and became underwater boulders. Kyle followed the curve of the harbor bowl, and the turtle was farther below him and getting deeper. There was resistance, and he swam harder. He lifted his head out and found himself in the merger line where the color of the water changed to navy, and the push of the real sea forced in choppy. The line of broken mountain tumbled into the water and broke the swells into riffles of white foam and spray. When he put his head underwater, the sea turtle was gone, and he could see across the ridge into a cobalt field of deeper water. Kyle kicked and pulled hard with his arms, trying to swim over the rocks and see what it was like on the other side. He fought against the moving water. He passed over the boulders. The drop-off knotted his stomach. There was nothing beyond the wall of rock, just a deep navy space that opened below his brown kicking legs. The ocean was real to him, the color of blueberry juice, and the power and mystery of it showed up inside him. He felt it. He imagined the viscous animals that he knew hunted underwater ledges, and he got nervous and wide-eyed behind the plastic pane of his diving mask. He brought his face out of the water and turned around, swimming on the surface toward the closest rocks.

The waves pushed him, and he came fast against the flat wet side of a boulder. Pinned there, he looked for a way to climb, and his bare feet hurt on the sharp edges he found below the water. He pulled himself up, spooked and imagining something coming for his legs at the last minute. He made his way through the rocks, slipping on the black water-beaten faces, tired and ready to get back to the beach. He stopped. He made himself stand up from his stooped crawling posture to look out at the sea and the coastline curving with greenery. The sun was getting low and turning flamingo. The hazy atmosphere magnified it, and the image trembled in the heat waves. He crossed the ridge and descended, sometimes having to sit on his wet swimsuit and scoot on a tilted plane of rock, back down to the calm harbor side where he lowered himself into the water and pushed off swimming again.

The shimmering material of his green swimsuit dripped, and he walked out of the water wiping his face and pressing the strip of black electrical tape. He could see his own wet eyelashes. They were pointed blurs, and looking past them was like looking out of a mouth filled with sharp teeth. Saltwater burned his eyes, and he tasted salt when he licked his lips. His heart beat in his chest, and the cut on his palm stung. He looked down at it, and it seemed like it stung because it was getting better. It seemed like the water was healing it. He had forgotten the cut. Sharks in Africa probably smelled the sharp fragrance of blood, he thought. Don sat beside the towel Kyle had left for himself on the beach. He wore long denim shorts, and he dug the heels of his leather sandals in the sand. He said something, but Kyle didn't hear him.

"What?" Kyle said.

"You didn't hear me?"

"No, I said 'what?'"

"I said, 'You made noises last night.' In your sleep."

"You heard me?"

"It was loud."

"I don't remember saying anything, really."

"No, you wouldn't. And you have tape on your shorts. Maunar and I are going out. Do you want to come?" Don threw the towel at Kyle. Kyle caught it at his chest and brought it up to bury his face in the orange, purple and blue stripes. He shook the folds out and wore the towel covering his head. He answered talking through the towel and moving his lips against it.

The salt and pepper tips of Manny's hair dragged across the burgundy upholstery in the back of his van. It was parked by the pay vacuums. All the doors were open, and the fat accordion hose lay on the oil-stained asphalt connected to a droning canister. Maunar recognized the desert scene airbrushed on the side of the brown van, and she pointed to it. They walked over and stood by the bumper and watched Manny move inside. The end of the hose sucked against the burgundy upholstery and changed its lay, and Manny didn't notice the three of them standing there. He worked shirtless and fast, circling himself and pivoting on his knee caps, his medallions swinging on their gold chains, and the black rope of alligator teeth bumped against his breastplate. The vacuum motor shut off, and Manny sat back on his folded legs and saw them standing there for the first time. Staring and blinking, "You almost scared me."

"Is this your van?" Don said

"Yeah, what are you doing here staring at me?"

"Seeing how long it would take for you to look up."

"How long did it take?" Manny said.

"A good while," Don said.

"How are you, Manny?" Maunar said.

"Oh the same as always."

"So pretty grumpy?" she said.

"Grumpy? I'm the best natured of any one of you. You don't mean that, little girlfriend."

"No, I'm just playing," she said, smiling and jutting her hips.

The gas station was full of people, and groups hung around outside and sat on cars, young people drawing with their fingers on each other's backs and standing up to act something out and sitting down again in cocked hats. There wasn't a free pump under the canopy. The instruction voice came loud from the self-serve speakers, and the feminine golem incanted the same prompts at different pumps at different times, like rounds recited by a congregation. The cars in the curved road used headlights, and people cruised in the cool twilight, listening to music, riding with the windows down. Subwoofers rattled trunks, and the town lights warped in the side panels that paraded in the congestion. Manny locked up his van and joined their party, and the four of them jaywalked between the bumpers of idle cars caught in a traffic jam. Their legs felt engine heat at the grills, and their skin lit in the headlight beams. They stepped over the chain sagging between posts and walked across the ditch through the coarse blades of grass to the gravel parking lot of the marina. The bars turned on their lights, and neon reflection snakes swam in the black marina water. Part of the sky still held a daylight look, and overhead was turquoise. An upside down sliver of moon descended beside a peach plane contrail that the atmosphere molded on one side, making it look toothed like a zipper across the sky.

The sky eased from her glow like a stripper. Heaven never rushed to her naked night. The tease caused more anticipation, and everyone bit his own stiff collar in the crackpot light that dissolved around him. The foreplay of twilight was the sky's promise. The village ahead had wraparound porches.

The music from inside melded with the street music. Excitement washed over them. Their strides adopted the oncoming beat, and the shaking started deep inside them. In the core of their bodies, they nestled a small vibration zone the size of a rolled up streamer. It was about to expand in each of them to the whole body. The frequency of the vibrations increased, and they were looking for everything.

Kyle's swimsuit was dry. It was short and rode high up his thighs when he climbed into a stool next to the balcony rail. He pulled them back down to the tan line, and Manny sat beside him and put the full pints of beer on the wooden rail. They looked out over the marina. The boats sat on the water like white swans backed up to the docks, and they read the names painted cursive on the sterns. Crews finished cleaning and hosing and slamming the lids of built-in coolers. They unloaded their hauls, stiff silvery needles in the halogen lamplight that buzzed stronger on wooden poles. Manny stretched for a plastic ashtray and lit a cigarette. They both sat there, Manny smoking, staring out at the marina, and Kyle thought about his day of walking and getting lost.

"So what's with the tape?" Manny said. He blew smoke out of his nose.

Kyle peeled back the tape and showed Manny the orange hologram. "I saw a special about how you shouldn't swim with any jewelry or anything that flashes. To a shark, it looks like fish scales or a wounded fish in the water."

"Boy you're crazy as hell. You're worried about something like that?" Manny patted the gold medallions hanging on his chest. "I swim with all these," he said. "If you're going to get eaten, it's not going to be because you got a shiny patch on your drawers."

Kyle restuck the strip of tape to his suit, and the orange hologram was covered. The tape adhesive was weaker, and the end curled. Kyle ran his finger over it, trying to smooth it down, and he picked up his beer and drank it, and he was thirsty from swimming. The beer was cold and fizzing in his mouth, the taste of wet static, and the frost on the glass melted and dripped tympanic where his swimsuit stretched to cover his lap. A dark ring of water soaked in the blanched wood, and he put the glass back on the rail in the same spot it had been in. He wiped the foam off his top lip with the pocket of his hand. "I'm just scared of sharks. I didn't used to be. I used to swim out past the sandbars with my family and nobody worried."

"You can't live your life in fear," Manny said.

"I can't help it. Now when I'm out there where I can't touch, I think about all the footage I've seen on cable, a shark just bombing in from out of no where."

"There's nothing as futile as regret. That's a famous quote."

"Who by?"

"Ah, it's a good quote, but look, I swim in cut off jeans. That's all I've ever swam in," Manny said.

"Yeah."

"I'll tell you, I'd be more afraid swimming with a bunch of women in the water than I would swimming with that hologram uncovered. Talk about a wounded fish."

Manny smoked his cigarette and drank his beer and looked across all the people sitting on stools at the high tables behind them. Don and Maunar shot pool by the wall. Don hovered low over the felt surface, and balls came together and touched each other, and one dropped away from view in the corner of the table. Don looked up into the row of lights and stood up, swinging his head around the tiffany panes that shaded the globes. Maunar watched him patrol the table looking for his next shot, and he rubbed the baulk line markers and tapped the veneer edge. She moved her hips in the shadows, dancing with her pool stick and singing along with the live music. The singer-songwriter wore a black hibiscus-print shirt and sang a mixture of covers and originals into the microphone under pink stage lights. A guitar curved over his thigh, and he hit high notes with his eyes closed, his teeth barred in a trimmed frame of chestnut goatee.

"I thought it was karaoke until I looked back there and saw the setup," Manny said, laughing.

People drank from fluorescent souvenir cups, curved like flower vases, stemmed and stamped with the grill logo. Rims were rocky with salt. Three girls tried to take a group picture of themselves with a camera phone unfolded and held at arm's length, as far away as possible. The dark shell of the phone pointed toward their packed in faces, and the display glowed white-blue in the other direction. Metal tacks pinned dollar bills to the wood along the bar shelves and support posts, and dollars hung taped to the low ceiling. Marker and pen covered the faces of the bills, drawings and messages, people's names and people who loved people. The bar got crowded. The roar of conversation lifted. Vacationers, dark from the sun, wore loud colors to contrast their new tans. Hot bodies gave back heat into the place, and they came to the bar to cut loose away from the eyes of home, and they were full of sun and drinks and sugar, crazy and healthy and carrying energy like bright batteries. Locals came out, too, to see the tourists and mix with them. Applause lifted in the room at the end of the song. "Thank you," the singer-songwriter said into the microphone. "I wrote that last one while I was in bed with a fever."

"Get well soon," someone yelled.

"Well I'm fine now," the singer said, and he chuckled and caused fuzzed distortion, overloading the microphone with an uncontrolled exhalation of breath, and the waitress, her T-shirt sleeves cuffed in baggy loops and her face covered in a thick mask of melted orange makeup, brought up the baskets of food they had ordered from the grill downstairs. Manny sucked his bottom lip over his lower teeth, and a shrill whistle beat the crowd roar down. Faces turned full toward them, and Kyle felt like all the sound went in his ear and no where else. He heard ringing. Don and Maunar hand-pocketed the remaining balls and walked away from the pool table. A stack of quarters sat on the rail, and a group of boys took up the sticks behind them.

Four baskets lined with wax paper nested fried fish on french fry beds, and the airy batter dissolved in their mouths leaving only the flakes of slick white fish to chew. Maunar held her fish basket on her tight lap of dark legs. The men leaned over their baskets balanced on the narrow rail, and a smooth cloud of wind-burnished gray moved low and rounded leading a gruesome parade of dark clouds toward the cluster of restaurants and bars around the marina. The light show started, and natural electricity flashed like rave strobes under the thick clouds. Lit like comic book backdrops, made unreal by the marina lights, they swirled maroon and brown, and the wall of rain came across the surface, firing into the black water and churning it white. The downpour gonged on the tin porch roof, and they ate watching a wall of water roll off in front of them. It splattered on the concrete dock below, and cool air from the upper atmosphere sank down with the curtains of rain and blew into their faces. The warm food went into their mouths and filled them up, and sensations ran up and down in their spines. The boats pitched, their bridges like scaffolding enclosed by clear plastic panels that took percussive hits of windblown water, and their tall antennas squirmed in the storm wind.

It calmed down to a sprinkle. Under a sheltered cleaning station, a deckhand finished fish for the people who chartered his captain. His curved fillet blade bent to run along the skeleton separating it from the skinless meat, and the people admired his work. Two pelicans floated in the dark underneath the shelter of the dock. The deckhand threw a handful over his shoulder without looking back, and the heavy gray and pink clumps separated in the air like sluggish shot and fell into the marina. The pelicans scooted across the surface of the rain-dimpled water, splashing with bowed wings until one threw its head back, its sack of throat rippling.

The storm passed. The steam bath aftermath issued from the sidewalk. The storm had dragged away any last hints of daylight, and left behind was a black night sky. Wet heat perspired in visible fog ropes. Haze hovered across the top of the water like a layer of feathers, and a vaporous mare's tail of wet white flame left the concrete under the halogen lights. The Bronco parked. Brake lights reddened the sauna. Diamondy, Zataurus, Slaw, Ralph, Honey, got out. Diamondy carried a duffel bag over his shoulder, and Zataurus's white suit blurred like a glamour shot in the emissions of mist. Across the band of dock, he straddled the gap between the concrete and the chrome strip embedded in the boat's gunwale. He pointed into the boat. He jerked at the leg of his pants flashing thin ankles, sockless above designer track shoes. Twinkling gold and green threads formed a crown stitched into the black leather shoe sides. He leaned over, and resting his forearm on his knee, he pointed directions. Everyone went aboard except Honey in her loose muumuu, damp above her swimsuit spots. Her wet ponytail hung in three heavy tendrils. Diamondy carried the duffel bag into the cabin of the boat, and through the windows, his head descended like a silent film's physical joke. Zataurus snapped his fingers at Slaw, and Slaw pulled up his puff-paint shirt and exposed a band of paisley boxers, a braided belt and a pair of sagging pockets. His arm disappeared to mid-forearm, and he brought out a cell phone. Slaw unfolded it and looked at the upper half. The display lit his face white-blue, shining on his teeth and glassing his eyes with glints. He dug into the button pad with his thumbs and then passed the phone to Zataurus who still stood spread between dock and fiberglass. He put the phone to the side of his face and waited. He never said anything. He folded the phone again.

They waited for the young captain. He appeared dark-bearded, and his hair was messed up. He hustled across the dock in a lime angler's shirt, deeply wrinkled, rubbing his face while he walked. He stepped aboard, and Zataurus eased his other leg over to the gunwale. He balanced on the balls of his feet while the young captain climbed the wet rungs of the chrome ladder. His boat shoes slipped on the rain-wet surfaces and rubbed against them, making noises like a handled balloon. At the top, he unzipped the plastic panel and crawled onto the bridge platform. He pulled himself up into the tall chair behind the wheel, and rumbling started. The sound of disturbed water rose up from the surface below the concrete dock edge. The young captain turned over his shoulder and yelled down, and Diamondy appeared again above board and yelled up to him. Diamondy came out to Slaw and punched him in the chest and grabbed him by the collarbone, and they all yelled back and forth up to the bridge and in each other's faces until Slaw jumped out onto the dock. He ran back to the Bronco, jumping the bellied chains at the parking lot edge. He brought two more nylon duffel bags out of the back hatch of the Bronco. Zataurus pivoted and swung his body around to balance facing the other way and watch Slaw. He shook his head. Diamondy went around the boat unmooring it from the top hat bollards, and the young captain at the wheel pushed on the throttle. Slaw sprinted. The duffel bags banged against his ribs. He jumped into the moving boat, and the engine changed tones again, and the water sounds increased. Honey waved. The boat moved forward, parting the wisps of steam, and the churn of white bubbled below. Zataurus balanced with both feet on the narrow boat back. Shirtless under his jacket, he put his hand under his lapel and patted his bare chest. Honey waved. In the middle of the marina, the young captain turned up the engine again, and the wake of white tail grew longer, and the stir of foam heightened. Water stacked on water. It aerated and blended, and the blades took the stillness out of the marina and made a salted froth of boiling activity. Honey switched hands and waved with the other one, and Zataurus unbuttoned his jacket, pushed the flaps back and held them open with his hands on his hips, his thumbs tucked inside his waistband. He was a decoration on the back of the boat, dressed to match the color of the fiberglass, a carved figuretail of masculinity. The young captain turned them through the gap between the two bell buoys and into the main drag where more restaurants lined the central channel, Tacky Jack's, Half Hitch, Wahoo Café. Nautical lights poured into the water. Port red and starboard green and basic white were festive reflections scattered in the warping black ripples. Honey waved. The figures stirred, pacing on the deck, silhouetted by the clean stark craft. Then the cabin lights came on. They waved, and the deck emptied, and Zataurus, too, was gone from his perch. Honey waved. The boat disappeared. The bell buoys bobbed with soused abrachia in the wake waves left behind, and Honey stood waving to nothing for a little bit.

Honey in the bar was shrink-wrapped in gold. The neon gases moved through their tubes behind the barstool she climbed into. She rotated. The bar stool swiveled. She spun around on it once, looking through the people, and the rotation was a change that outlined an origin no one else had. The muumuu hid a sweet genius that paled the spiritual lights of everyone else in the room, and they were all flashlights in the daytime compared to her, and each strand of blond was a filament, so her hair was halation, blurred at the edges of her form. The way she looked was different. She was a different color, like the particles inside her were imported from the shifting bed of an edenic estuary, charged with static that drew attractiveness and reissued it into the room endued with her own unique flavors. He picked up transmissions from her, and he imagined them as spheres of sonicating aura dressed in little peasant smocks, and they wore extraterrestrial feathers in their hair, and a collection of truth riddles looked out from her face. Trying to solve them felt like the meeting of sable and skin. Looking at her caused unrest in him, like the idea of certain fabrics touching each other, like the doctor of magic whispered a silk band down his throat. He watched her from across the room, and he gagged and lost his throat thinking of a series of textures. He saw her arm on the shellacked oak bar when she turned and ordered from the bartender. He licked the inside of his mouth, and the texture thoughts made him really shake his head in the bar, and he thought of it again for the effect it caused in him, and he shook his head again, his curls soft-bumping his temples, and he found himself making his way across the room to her. He went a way in the maze where two chairs backed up to each other, touching, blocking the route. He had to turn around and go another way. Honey had an effect on him. He walked up to her. She was right there next to him. Her drink came. It was foggy in a tall glass cylinder, and mint leaves stuck out the top.

"What's that? What's that drink?"

"I was with this couple once, back home, my girlfriend and her boyfriend. The three of us were in a video store. We had been out drinking, and he kept trying to pull her shirt up. She didn't have a bra on. People could have seen her chest, and every time he would try to pull her shirt up, he would yell, 'Mojitos!'"

"What is mojitos?"

"That's what this drink is. Man, please tell me my little story wasn't so boring you forgot you asked me a question."

"You think about that story every time you order the drink?"

"I order the drink so I will think about the story, yeah, and not only do I think about it, I can barely order without laughing."

"Where was this story?"

"Back home, Florida," she said.

"I love Florida."

"You from there?"

"No, I'm from Georgia, but we go to Florida all the time."

"Even in the winter?"

"I went in October once," he said.

"I guess you love Florida."

"Yeah, the beach was strange in October. People had all their

Halloween decorations out, like cobwebs hanging in the condo windows, and jack-o-lanterns in the palm tree courtyards. It was funny."

"And all the vampires were too tan to suit you?" she said.

The bartender walked by scanning the glasses and bottles and faces at the bar. Kyle made eye contact with him, and the bartender lifted his chin. "I'll try one of those," Kyle said, pointing to her mojito. The bartender turned and started mixing. "What's in one?" he said.

"I don't know," she said. "You can try mine. You've already ordered it though, so I guess it doesn't matter whether you like it or not." He took her glass and pinned the black straw to the rim with his finger and drank straight out of the glass. His nose nestled into the leafy mint sprigs. "You can use my straw," she said.

"It's good. I'm glad I'm getting one. What's your name?"

"Honey. What's yours?"

"Kyle."

"For real?" she said.

"Right, that's what I was about to ask you. My name's real, yeah."

"Mine, too," she said, sucking mojito through her straw, her face half-blue in the neon sign light.

"No, I don't think so," he said, laughing.

"That's what everyone calls me here."

"What do they call you at home in Florida?"

"It doesn't matter cause we're not in Florida. I'm Honey here."

"That's sort of mysterious," he said.

The bartender put down a cocktail napkin and a plastic cup filled with the foggy fluid, and mint leaves crowded the opening. "Sorry we ran out of glasses," he said. "Three." He held up his fingers. Kyle brought out his credit card and passed it over the bar to the bartender.

"Want to keep it open?"

"Sure," he said.

They drank mojitos, and Honey's came in plastic cups, too, now. They talked close and loud to hear each other. A different band took the stage, a group of young men in tight tattered jeans and long braided hair, touring from Brooklyn. The lead singer wore a vest, and ribbons above his elbows cinched his cream renaissance sleeves. His eyes were dark with eyeliner, and they draped a string of white lights across their set. Their voices warbled and harmonized over the music, thumping and swaggering. The shtick of a midnight marching band in romantic lights, the femininity of the bulbs reproduced in the kit braces and elongated in the lacquered brass of the trumpet player's curved bell. Hand claps and bottle banging. The trombone player wandered off the stage blowing his part with puffed cheeks and walking through the crowd. At the rail, his slide extended and hung in the air over nothing. Kyle's throat ached. He took ice in his mouth and bit down on it. His teeth were cold, and he couldn't feel them with his numb tongue. A gang of people walled them in at the bar and ordered over their heads. Drinks and hands passed in front of their faces, and they smelled money. Kyle chewed a mint leaf on purpose. He wanted to taste it. He got funny looks. They slinked out and walked down the steep wooden staircase with three full cups of mojito.

They found Don and Maunar sitting in an aluminum jon boat that sat aground in the flower bed as an ornamental display. The name of the grill was painted on the bow. Manny stood across the platform of dock tearing crackers from their packets and dropping the pieces into the marina between boats. "He claims he saw a tarpon," Maunar said. "All I saw were little minnows."

"I saw a tarpon," Manny said.

"Is this your crowd? Hi, I'm Honey."

"I work with them. Manny, Maunar and Don," Kyle said, pointing them out.

Don lifted his head out of his hands. "Nice to meet you. Are you cool here? Cause Manny isn't."

"I'm just a little antsy." He threw a saltine in the water.

"He actually wants to drive us back to the hotel to see that big deal wedding reception."

"There it was again," Manny said. "A whole section of his dorsal fin just came out of the water. It was huge. You heard the splash, right?" Manny said. Honey walked over to the edge and looked into the water with Manny. Kyle followed her, and Don and Maunar stood up in the bedded jon boat. They stepped out of it into the black soil and bark and walked across the platform. They all stared down at the water. Manny dug in the pocket of his denim cutoffs and pulled out another pack of saltine crackers. The squares were already crumbled in the red, blue and clear wrapper, and Manny frowned trying to rip the plastic open with his fingers.

"You want to go to a wedding reception?" Honey said.

"Yeah, it'll be fun," Manny said, fumbling and turning the pack in his hand trying to open it at a different side. "It's too crowded here, and the band's too loud and weird."

"I just met you, but you don't seem like the type that would like wedding receptions," she said.

"This one's different," he said. "Here, see if you can't get these crackers open, little girlfriend." He gave her the cracker pack and pulled two more out from his pocket. Kyle put the mojitos down in a row on the dock and took a cracker pack, too. They broke the saltines that weren't already crushed and threw the bits onto a patch of the black water where the purple oil sheen had been broken up by the feeding cigar minnows. They went after the crackers, and the crackers spun and skated pale on the dark-tinted surface.

"I need to go close my tab if we're leaving," Kyle said.

"Shh, just wait," Manny said, putting his arm around their shoulders and pulling them in close together. "Just wait," he said, and they all stood, huddled and watching. The pieces floated and expanded to absorb the inky water, and the minnows kept working on them, breaking them up, hitting them and nibbling bits into smaller pieces of swollen crumb and snatching them underwater, the tiny frenzy playing out like toy violence in a circle of bunted plashes, and segments of their black and rainbow bodies flashed at the surface in a dance of plops, rotating into tiny whirlpools that spun as if stirred by the pates of pirouetting figurines on a submerged music box. The first part of a tinny song hissed and wobbled out from the bar sounding like comb-stroked holes punched in a spinning cylinder. Then the bass drum exploded a thunder of grumbles, and the music was bigger than the playing fish. It was no longer their soundtrack. The chorus could have come from the dark storm clouds that stalled on the other side of the island.

F olding tables and chairs covered the beach behind the hotel. They had been brought in during the storms and set up a second time just before the reception. Strung up jars gave candlelight through their colored shapes, and a centerpiece of flowers huddled on each white tablecloth. Tea candles floated in crystal bowls filled with water, and rich light warmed the faces of the guests sitting down having the meal, and others milled and mixed, standing in the white sand with gold wine or squatting beside other tables, squeezing arms and patting backs. The women wore sequins and piebald prints. Taffeta gulped the sea breezes, and the men wore dark suits and starched shirts. The groom was from a Middle Eastern oil family. His party had black hair tinged with purple, and the bride was from Chicago. The serving tables were set up at the end of the beach, and the waitstaff comported in white coats behind the spreads, keeping the presentations pretty through second helpings. Silver bell-top servers stood on ornate legs, and warming canisters underneath whispered heat up to the dishes, and blossoms had been carved out of the watermelon meat. Cubes of cheese and star-cut pineapple tumbled out of a tall mallow arrangement. "Hey Honey, you know back there at the bar when you asked me whether or not I liked wedding receptions?" Manny said.

"Yeah?"

"I should have said, 'I liked all three of mine.'"

"That would've been funny," Maunar said.

The father of the groom walked across the seawall. His champagne ran with fizz columns, and he held his glass up to the microphone and touched the rim with a spoon. Ringing was amplified by the speakers stacked in the rolling cabinet, and the guests' talk died down. The wait staff filed in through the tables. Everyone took champagne flutes from the trays, and the groom's father started a speech, and Manny led them down the concrete steps while he talked. They moved at the reception fringe toward the table designated as the open bar. Rick from Colorado tended. His black bowtie was crooked, and the metal clips fastening it to the collar showed. He whispered with his wide hot face and slipped them beers that had been floating in a tub of ice water. They crouched down and drank them at the back edge of the party. The sand was cool from the rain, but it was already dry. The father tried to embarrass the groom with humiliating childhood stories. Kyle located the head table, looking through the faces and bodies. The groom was handsome with white teeth and a straight face. His hair looked crunchy with gel, and it was messed up just right. The bride beside him wore shimmering white, and she was pretty with a brilliant hooked nose, and her eyes sported a rascal's spark. She jabbed and laughed at him during the story, and he mantled his hand across his brow. Volleys of low laughter rolled through the party tables, and the father spoke with a heavy accent. He built the story to its climax. "All with a sudden, he burst at the room with just the underpants and a cape for a towel," he said, and everyone laughed. He saluted the couple and raised his glass above his head. All the glasses were raised, and all the glasses clinked.

Kyle touched the neck of his wet beer bottle to Honey's, and sand stuck to the deep amber glass. He put his bottle back down in the sand, building a cup holder to steady it. He wiped his hands on his green swimsuit.

Honey sat beside him, her body curled up inside the wild muumuu that stretched over her knees and tented her hidden. She hugged her legs, and he looked down her armholes for her body. Her untanned sides show pale in the shadows. She looked relaxed, and her blond hair twisted in the sticky night air. Wisps floated. Humidity fuzzed the helices that tumbled down her back and down her brown arms, and she looked messy like she had just woken up in God's favorite meadow. She was like a cute animal who didn't even know about looks, good or bad, and she smiled about the toast and the foreign father's superhero story. Her canine overlapped her incisor, and her lip stuck to the crooked tooth. Kyle stared at her trying to figure her mouth out. Twitches fired in different parts of her upper lip, and she turned to him and didn't say anything. He kept looking, and she looked back at him, and it was comfortable for them to stare at each other. Her face changed every few seconds, and he didn't understand it. Her mouth moved, but nothing came out. Her lips were loose, and her wet teeth were back behind them in the beginning of her mouth. Kyle finally broke the stare and looked over at the waves sloshing up on the glass pane of white sand, and he looked at his lap, and he looked up. She scooted over, moving closer to him. The frilled muumuu fringe gathered by his leg, and he felt her thigh against his.

The entertainers had painted faces. Stripes of their own skin showed up mahogany under the red and blue swirls, and they were half-dressed in swaddling napkins or second hand fandango gear. They lit torches on the stage and straddled drums. The wooden shells at their humanity, they palm-beat and finger-whipped the taut heads, dirt-smeared with use, and they took the concrete stage of seawall like a crazed gang of psychopomps, hand-springing and pronating, some of them jumping off the seawall into the sand, crab-walking and joker-jumping through the tables, and their cartwheels caused sand bursts and shrill yammering. Their tongues mauled the ridged roofs of their mouths, and rhythms took over heartbeats, and everyone stared at the arrival. Shining eyeballs reflected torchlight, and the party underwent sublimation, so the members were instantly transported midway to euphoria, and a curled red fetus was painted on the belly of a man whose face was half blue, and he wore bright red lipstick. The ambit of the rite jostled their heads loose on their necks and rolled their eyes sloshed in their heads like upset ball compasses, and a man on stilts came out wearing enormous bell bottoms and streamers tied around his neck. He danced tall. He jerked a man off the concrete, jolting a knot in the nodular limbus of his arm joint. He threw him to a standstill on the shoulders of another man who tossed him into a back flip off the seawall, and he landed fitful in the sand. The contortionist stole the veil from the bride, wore it on his own head, and black dreads shook behind the fall of tulle. He jacked his limbs and mutated himself, wobbling across the stage on his palms with his legs hooked over his shoulders, and his pendulum of bottom swung like a diapered thorax. The pseudo ringmaster in a grape top hat and tails skipped out, and the peacock feather, stuck in the silk band, arced behind him forever. He turned into a handstand and stood on one palm, doffing the hat and spreading his legs upside down to conjure a scatterbrained starfish. The feather whipped the ground and convected a layer of dust, and the whole crew joined in the center and flipped in unison. Symmetry developed in the gymnastics until the jumping leader came to the forefront, lurching ahead and rearing back with nylons webbed between his fingers. A stationary routine came over him, and his ankles seemed spring-loaded during a series of twisting flips. The girls ran out onto the seawall with fruits and cones tied to their hair ends, dragging down their piles, and they stomped and promenaded in a conga line, chanting treble verses of jaw-riding poetry, and their painted pinafores flapped in their throes like bird wings over their scrimp-cut gym shorts. Then the fire breather came out.

"What did I tell you?" Manny said. "This isn't an ordinary wedding reception."

Kyle found his hand on Honey. She took it in her lap watching the act. Neither of them looked directly at the pairing but sidelong, and both were conscious of the connection, making slight movements to rerev the thrill of touch. Rows of people sat down in the sand at the start of the show, and everyone inched up among the children who watched in front with their hands buried in the sand. Manny and Don and Maunar crouched behind them to see, too, and they passed more beers forward.

The fire breather lit his skewer off one of the existing torches and crouched down on the seawall with his back to the beach and tables. He blew a fireball down into the concrete, and it rolled upwards around his body, hiding him in a blossom of bonfire like an ephemeral ground rose, and he reappeared flipping out of it and off the seawall, landing in the sand. Fire came from his mouth and up into the sky, and he blew with a brass player's embouchure, sputtering mists that sparked and dissolved in free-fall, and he tramped bandy-legged in front of the tables, blasting flames and painting the air with twisted ropes of white heat. He breathed fire onto a second skewer, and it took the flame, an auxiliary torch, and arching backwards like a limbo jock, he hovered the first lit skewer over his face and lowered the light into the red interior of his wet mouth. He shut his lips around the skewer's shaft, and the fire was gone. He stood up rubbing his torso. He had eaten the fire. He smiled and wiped the orange curlicues of burning cinder out of his beard, and the smell of human hair was left in the wind wake of the fire eater, sprinting across the beach and spouting quick blasts. He panted visible fire barks before putting a dreadlock in his mouth to soak away the remnant paraffin. Then he took a plastic bottle out of his back pocket and guzzled it to refuel. He spewed some at the skewer, blowing a foxtail into the night sky, and the faces closest to him took the energy in light form. A small nocturnal sun exploded, and a roaring suck of engulfed air sounded like a wind-whipped banner. The breather's little body was compact and wiry with black nubs of chest hair, and his abdomen shone slick with perspiration in the lurid light of the new heavens he unfurled. He spoke to the crowd in a hot tongue, rich with energy. The oilmen and the Illinoisans both followed the pyrotechnical glossolalia, seeing shapes in the fire pillars he blew, and the new union of flesh was already on everyone's mind, so the flames put some tuned ones in a prophetic mood, and they searched for pyromantic pictures of the new couple in the flares.

A big man sat turned with his arm hooked over the back of his chair.

He smoked a handsome cigar, and the fire breather trotted over pantomiming an offer to intensify his light. The man belly-laughed and giggled smoke. The crowd laughed, and the fire eater shuffled sideways scanning them for more interaction, and he squatted facing Kyle. "Open your mouth," the fire eater said, and he stood hunkered, splayfooted in the sand with the lit skewer drawn back like a short javelin. Up close, his cheeks were cracked and scaly, and his whole face was powdered with ash. The burned particles in his beard fused the melted curls, and the growth hung like grizzled moss from his face. "Open your mouth," the fire eater said. The words were slurred, and he gargled paraffin to talk.

"What?"

"Open your mouth," the fire eater said.

Kyle stood up tall on his knees, tilted his head back and opened his mouth. The fire eater lowered the skewer and brought it down to his face. Kyle stared up at the flame coming toward him, and he felt the heat on his eyebrows and the bridge of his nose, and then he fell back in the sand, confused and falling into Honey.

"What happened?" Kyle said.

"He was about to stick the fire in your face," Honey said.

"But what happened? Did I fall?"

"I pulled you down by the shirttail."

"Oh man, I didn't feel that."

"He looked crazy, like he was about to really do it," she said.

The fire eater hopped in reeling turns. He jumped, grabbing the top of the seawall, pulling himself up. Standing on the ledge, he bent over and gave a final breath of flame backwards through his legs. The people cheered and clapped.

Don stood up behind them, and he gripped Kyle's shoulder. "Rickarado's saying no more beers down here. Come on and help me get some more."

The reception spread out. Don and Kyle found members of the wedding party smoking cigarettes by the glowing blue lagoon of pool. Water scattered the spotlight that shone from the deep-end wall, and shallow channels ran on either side of the parterre island to another lit deep-end, where girls in dresses stood testing the spring of the diving board, advancing toward the end and retreating again. Groomsmen wearing bruised boutonnieres gathered around bridesmaids who sat upright in the chaise lounges, tugging at the armpits of their hot salmon tube tops and sucking on their cell phone antennas.

Kyle followed Don cradling a large paper bag of cold twelve packs they found in the industrial-sized kitchen refrigerator. Don stopped on the pool deck and put his fingernails against Kyle's shirt. "Hold on, we got something starting here," he said, and they sat down on a tiled wall that enclosed an elevated flower bed. Striped plant tips slipped into their collars. Don pointed out a man in a khaki suit who gestured to the group around him, and the man's voice grew louder coming from his bone-plated face. Another young guy tried to keep things light and tousle his sandy hair stalks, but the athlete averted and slapped his wrist and said, "I can. I swear to you, I can. I was an Olympic athlete. I competed in the long jump. You honestly don't think I can jump from here to that island?"

"No, I don't think you can."

"These were the real Olympics you, uh, were a competer?"

"Competitor."

"The real Olympics," the athlete said, and he pulled his wallet out of his inside coat pocket and dug through the leather flaps. "I have here a laminated participant's badge from Barcelona 1992."

Don passed a beer to Kyle and took one out of the paper bag for himself. He rolled it closed again. "Reality is entertaining, and it seems like I always have a front row seat," Don said.

"You're always really looking around?"

"Yeah, I think he might could do it."

"It seems like I could. I know I could get three quarters across," Kyle said.

"It's farther than it looks," Don said. "Hey, I saw you two getting pretty familiar down there."

Kyle laughed and hung his head.

"Where'd she come from?"

"It's weird, Don, I saw her in the woods earlier today after I left your place. She was at this old house on the mountain, walking around without a top in front of all these guys. It didn't seem like she was half-naked though. Her body was so put together and tight, and nothing was hanging. She looked like art or a statue. She didn't see me cause I was hiding back in the trees, but then the crazy thing is she just came into the bar tonight. I thought I'd never see her again, and then there she was."

"I saw her on the dock with Zataurus. Did you see that?"

"Yeah, the guy in the white suit. Who's he?"

"I wanted to warn you about him. He's a drug runner. Comes from a long line of drug runners, infamous guys on the island. He's a serious type. He can get pretty scary, and if she's his, I wouldn't advise asking to loan her out."

"His?"

"Yeah, his. He was in the class below mine in school. Both things and people become his real fast if he wants them."

"And you think she's his?"

"She told you her name is Honey?"

"I know. I know. It's a pet name."

"And pets are property," Don said. "Look, all I know is that it's smart to know whose hand you're holding."

"Do you think drug runners are the new pirates?" Kyle said.

Don shrugged. "Could be."

The Olympic athlete took his sport coat off and laid it across the foot of an empty chaise lounge. He sat down and unlaced his wingtips, and he pulled his bare feet out of argyle socks. He stripped down to his white undershirt, untucked it and emptied his pockets. He stretched his legs and rolled his head and paced, padding around on the pumice pool deck while the bet money was collected from everyone involved. The wad was given to a bridesmaid. She straightened the money and fanned it and refolded it. She shoved it into her tube top and pulled it out again, "I'm just playing. No," she said. "I'll leave it lying right here in my lap. I promise. And I won't let anyone touch it."

"Why does she need to hold it?" someone said. "His whole wallet's right there on the chair if we wanted it."

The athlete cleared a passage through the empty chaise lounges and backed up against the concrete balustrade. He took deep breaths and started his approach, sprinting across the deck, slapping the pumice with his toes. The long penultimate stride and the shorter last, he took off high across the pool channel, cycling his legs and running in midair. He shorted it and had to break form and land with one foot making it onto the island and the other kicking into the water.

"He made it," the bridesmaid said.

"Oh no, we didn't discuss a botched landing," someone said.

"Special Olympics."

The athlete stood up and pulled his wet leg out of the pool. His heavy pants stuck to him and dripped. He took them off and his undershirt, wadded them and threw them across the pool channel. He jumped in and swam toward the lit deep-end, playing and splashing in his duck-print boxers.

Honey and Kyle walked to the wave breaks, down the beach away from the party. In the dark, the sand sparked with blue-green phosphorescence under their steps, and they walked on the stars reflected in the sea-washed slick of low-tide grains. Tiny balls of water flew under the semicircle horn of moonlight, and they were by themselves under the peach and blue parenthesis of hovering crystals. The rental catamarans were dragged close together around a stand of palm trunks and shrubs, and she took his hand and pulled him up the sea-bitten ledge, across the silver sugar of beach and into the trees. They climbed over the white hulls and sat down on the stretched canvas platform of a catamaran at the back of the grove. It had been shoved into the sea daisy and joewood brambles at the base of the mountain slope, and they sat there next to the curling bush twigs, looking out from the shadows through the bars of black trunk toward the beach. It looked lighter now that they were in a darker dark, and the scene was incised on the metal night. Harbor water floated platinum shavings from the hotel's lampposts, and the sterling blue water had looked black to them before when they sat near the torches. Now they saw in different colors, and in a parade of retreating settings, they could know everything in a different way. Some animal crawled through the dry leaf bed of the thick behind them.

Kyle looked down, and she dug through her leather pocketbook. Paper rattled inside the pouches. Objects touched each other. She brought out a rubber band with gold foil woven into the black sheath, stretched it around her fingers and gathered her hair into a ponytail. She moved her purse across the canvas, leaning over his lap. He smelled her neck, and it was in his face, and he kissed the blond skin and the little curls. She came toward him with her face, and her head was tilted with lowered lids, and she got close and blurred.

In the low visibility, her mouth hung loose, and he felt her hot breath go into his mouth. The sensations were new, and he felt them in his brain. They kissed in the dark, and they got used to the dark. Their eyes adjusted. Night vision came on, and their shapes took on definition in each other's eyes. The grayness in front of him missed pins of light, and their belladonna eyes were dilated like obsidian coins.

The lamp on his dresser was from home. He clicked it on in his small room, and the forest-green shade controlled the bulb. They squinted. Shine ran up the paneling, and a wave of home feeling flashed through him after seeing the lamp, its white ceramic base and the painted red cardinal sitting on a section of pine limb. The cardinal was a male. It was top-knotted, and his mother had wrapped the lamp in newspaper and put it in the bottom of his suitcase for him. The lamp meant home, the way he meant home to his mother, and she wanted him to remember the things he liked about Georgia, the lake in the backyard and the birds and the fires and the pine islands, the drainage pipes he spray-painted and streaked with firework sulfur. The root-buckled driveway was good for bike tricks. She kissed him. He saw her face, and they dragged each other, kicking ankles and feet, and they crashed into the table. The brick bookends fell over and books fell over, and she breathed and backed herself in another direction, pulling him toward the bed. He snatched the old photo of Julie off the nail so Honey wouldn't see it. It fell into the corner of the room. The mattress springs moaned. He crawled over her with a knee between her legs, and they aligned their bodies, and their places pressed against each other. They rolled back and forth letting gravity change the pressure. The muumuu came up and destroyed her hair into a huge tangled pile, and they had to part it to find each other's faces again. They concentrated on the lips and only scanned each other with their peripheral vision, afraid to gawk and study and revel in the nakedness like they wanted to. Then she rolled over, and he focused his eyes on the back of her arm. The mandala of freckles there held a sacred space. Getting to her back and facing him again, her cheeks flickered with reaction. Her nose bridge was sun-splotched. Her upper lip twitched and changed, and moisture balls sat in the blond hairs. Her lips were salty and sunburned with discolorations of hot pink and red.

The television picked up a rerun game show. They had the volume knob turned down, and the picture fuzzed in and out with static. They used it as a blue nightlight in the room. They talked and looked at the screen, the old hairstyles and the velvet set, touching each other under the thin sheets with just fingertips, and the effleurage sent cold chills through their spines. The box fan blew directly on them. Kyle's sentences slowed down, and his blinks lasted longer. He felt sleep welling up in him. It felt like his eyes were painted shut, like heavy oils depicted a drunken midnight choir on the skin of his eyelids. Honey turned toward him and propped herself up on her elbow.

"Are we going to send out a search party for your eyes?" she said.

"Maybe. I can't see them," he said. He looked at her.

"You look tired. Your eyes are leaving me."

"I don't want to close them though."

"It's alright. Go to sleep, funny prince."

K yle dreamed he sat on the beach with Honey. The beach wasn't on the island. It was a cold beach somewhere else, maybe in California. The sand was brown, and there were smooth pebbles mixed in with the grains. A red and white bell buoy bobbed in the water behind the white caps. They sat next to each other looking at it sway back and forth in the water, and the bell rang, and the water was a pretty royal color. Kyle wanted to go in, but he was wearing casual clothes, and he knew the water was too cold. Even the breeze was cold that came in from the ocean.

"How do you spell 'buoy'?" Honey said.

Kyle tried to spell it several times for her, but he couldn't. He kept messing up and starting over, and he wasn't even sure he knew how to spell the word, but he wanted to impress her. He kept trying. A voice came from behind. "Did you say b.y.o.b.?" A group of surfers and young men ran up with boards and coolers and transistor radios. They circled Kyle and Honey in the sand, partying around them, dancing and bopping a beach ball through the air. One of the boys took Honey's hand and tried to pull her up to party with them. Honey screamed and resisted. She punched the boy's wrists. Kyle got to his feet and pushed them, but they stayed in the same place, dancing and partying without noticing him.

He came out of the dream and opened his eyes. Honey was asleep beside him, and she hugged her pillow instead of resting her head on it. She was puffy and loose-faced with deep sleep. He sat up in bed and leaned over to see the red numbers of the alarm clock on the floor. He was awake because of the fight dream, and he didn't want to try falling asleep again. The television was completely filled with static now, and he crawled over her without making any noise. He felt like walking in the predawn with the world all to himself. He wanted to think about all that had happened in such a short amount of time and be proud of himself. He probably felt different, but he hadn't had time to notice, and he wanted to go out before the sun came up giving its attitude to a new day. She would need her car eventually, and he could walk to the marina to get it for her. He could walk to the marina and think, and there wouldn't be anyone out so early, he thought. He could walk down the middle of the road if he wanted to. Then they could ride together to a breakfast place when she woke up, and maybe she knew of one where there was a patio where they could sit outside and drink coffee in the shade. There was a lot of the island he hadn't seen yet. She could be his tour guide and ride him around with vents blowing on bi-level to cool his face and his feet at the same time. He was excited about another day. The more he woke up, the more excited he was, and he wondered if she drank coffee.

Her leather pocketbook sat on the dresser. He held it unzipped next to the glowing screen so he could see inside. The static showed rubber bands for hair, and detached strands tangled around an ink pen's clip. There was a round tin of lip dew. Receipts rattled when he put his hand inside. The pocketbook was crowded, and he felt the keys in the bottom among coins. He pulled them out and put the pocketbook back on the dresser where it had been. He opened the door and propped it with his foot. Pressing the button in on the inside, it clicked flush with the metal knob. The world wasn't alive. Lights that always stayed on poured from the bathhouse door and the vents above.

"What are you doing?" She moved under the sheets, and her head lifted.

"I was going to walk to get your car for you."

"Don't do that. Come back to bed."

"You'll need it eventually."

"But not right now. We'll get it tomorrow."

"It's tomorrow already. I can't sleep anymore."

"Please get back in here with me," she said. "Get back in bed."

He crawled over her and lay on his back looking at the electric snow light the television put on the wall beside him. She slung her arm across his chest and went back into the slow breathing of deep sleep. He was awake, and he felt awake, but he closed his eyes and listened to her breathing. He listened to the drone of the fan motor, and he did his method for getting to sleep. He let pictures come into his head, and he left them there and didn't think about anything except seeing the pictures and focusing on them no matter what they were. He saw a girl in a green dress standing in the middle of a redwood forest. He focused on it, and the picture changed. The same girl levitated above his head with her dress like a bell and her legs the hanging clappers. She looked Polynesian. His mind moved the picture, and it changed into another picture, a close-up of the flower she wore in her hair. Flat, armored bugs crawled out of the red throat, across the petals toward her jet black hair. There was panic with the picture. He saw a boy punting a glass jar, and he felt a sleepy feeling. He saw black letters spelling DURANGO, three dimensional in solid whiteness. A lanky cheetah wore sunglasses and lay stretched out on top of the word. A monster truck hung in the middle of a packed arena. The fenders were painted with teeth. Flames breathed from the exposed block, and flashbulbs fired in the stands.

She read one of his novels out loud to him on the beach after the sun came up, and not many people were out so early. Her voice was soft and sweet, and she was easy to listen to. She read with a good rhythm, and it was like she was talking to him and telling a story in a natural way. She didn't stumble over very many words. When she did, she laughed and excused herself and kept reading. The harbor was still and facing up like a vanity mirror reflecting the sky's morning colors, pink, pale, and the clouds were airbags filled with glowing gases. The sun came over the mountain and hit him in the ribs, and the sand divided into day-white mounds and dawn-blue divots in the angled light. Porcelain crabs ran and froze while she read, their carapaces a dingy yellow like statues in ruin and their wrists like can openers, floating over the talcum powder sand with transparent leg movements that blurred like heat waves. The sun climbed higher, cutting into the sky with razor rays and eclipsing the feel of morning. She lay on her stomach, propped on her elbows to read. She lifted her leg and dropped it down, and her toe drove into the sand. She wiggled her foot to bury it hidden. Kyle watched the light beating down on her back, and he touched the lower part where little blond hair grew arranged in a line that pointed down toward her hot pink bikini waist. Her skin was warm and brown, and she got to the end of a chapter.

They walked into the harbor together, holding hands and kicking encased sea beans through the clear water. Waves washed up around their ankles, and the folding suck hollowed out a space under the arches of their feet. It dug terraces in the moving mixture of sediment and shell chips. Empurpled auger bits, knotted flamingo tongues and chipped tivella shells rolled across their feet, and they walked in, stepping down each ledge and getting deeper in bursts like walking down stage risers. Kyle's swimsuit ballooned with air in the front, and Honey batted the inflation with the flat of her hand. He buckled his knees, and bubbles came out of his leg holes and broke on the surface. He floated on his back, dipping his hair wet and looking back at the swells to ride himself over them. Honey swam to him and latched onto his torso. He righted himself touching the bottom with the toes of his pointed feet, and she wrapped herself around him like a panda bear, her wet face in front of him. Her breath was salty, and all the twists were dragged out of her hair by the water weight, so he could see the true shape of her head. It was old-fashioned, the intelligent dome of royalty, and he bobbed and balleted in the swells holding her, and some waves were big enough to lift them. He dog paddled farther and wore her like a living vest. "You don't swim?" he said.

"Not when I have a beautiful boy to hang onto."

Out where he couldn't touch, the swells topped their heads, and the turquoise water surrounded them and floated their hair and swayed it like submerged grasses. Bands of light scanned them, baptismal photocopiers that reproduced their selves. They stared at each other underwater, weightless and conjoined like fetal friends in the warm font of the harbor. They pulled elastic in the Sunday sea. It hosted their act and married them, and they added their personal salts to the ancient mixture. Kyle looked up through the water to the morning sun dancing on the surface above. Globular light broke apart and reformed. The buoyancy cradled them and brought them to the surface again. They were pushed back toward shore, and their heels scraped bottom. Gasping and blowing, water drained from their ears, and the foaming breaks were louder in a pop of fluid suction. They looked to see if anyone had seen them swimming.

"Do you want me to keep reading?" she said. She turned the pages trying to find the place she left off. Her wet fingers soaked water into the yellowed pages of the paperback, and Kyle smelled the old smell of the open book blowing by him in the wind. Honey wiped her face with the towel and licked her lips, getting ready to read again. Hemispheres of water evaporated off their skin, and Kyle lay on his back with his eyes closed, listening to the story and the waves. He didn't follow the story but heard the words as daydream inducers, and his mind caught on phrases and ran with them. The sun came up higher and shone through his lids and lit them orange in front of his eyes. His hand searched across their towels. Without looking where he felt, he found Honey's towel and then her damp suit and side. He touched her thin forearm, and she dropped the book with that hand and touched him back and kept reading. He rubbed her palm with his thumb and touched each of her fingers with his eyes shut. "Is this your hand?" he said.

She finished the paragraph. "The one you're holding? Open your eyes if you want to know things."

"Sorry," he said. "I don't mean to stop the chapter, but what about Zataurus?"

"Zataurus?"

"Zataurus," he said.

Yeah, I live at his house. I work for him."

"You don't date him, do you?"

"You mean like go out on dates to the movies or the butterfly farm?"

"I don't know about that. Are you involved with him?"

He turned over on his stomach and put his shirt on top of his head. She looked at the pages of the book. "He just sort of found me," she said. "I came down here last summer like you did, and when he found me, it was August, and I wasn't really sure whether I wanted to go back home or not. There were classes and home stuff, and he just made the choice extra easy."

"You mean he kidnapped you?"

She let go of his hand, rolled away to the other edge of her towel and put her eyes in the crook of her arm.

"Honey?" he said. "What's your real name? Do you like living there with him? Just tell me. I'm interested. I want to know."

"It's not a kidnapping if you wanted to be stolen."

"Do you ever do anything you don't want to do?"

"You mean, do we sleep together?"

"Okay, alright."

"No, he always moves to the couch on the porch afterwards. He likes the night air better, especially when there's a storm."

"What?"

"I'm kidding," she said. "I don't do anything I don't want to do. He's good to me. I live there for free. I'm just their little mascot. I'm just the girl. I provide a little feminine relief, and I keep the place straight. Everybody's happy."

"But would he be good to you if he knew you were here right now doing this? And would he be good to me? There's the question. I have a right to know that at least."

"I've never done anything like this before, so I don't know. But generally, I'm a private person."

"Honey, I saw you before we met at the bar last night," he said. "I've been meaning to bring it up. I saw you earlier yesterday."

"At the grocery store?"

"No, did you go to the grocery store yesterday?"

"In the morning. I bought canned pineapple for sandwiches."

"That sounds good, but look, I saw you in the afternoon at the big white house on the mountain, and you didn't have your top on in front of all those guys. That doesn't sound too private to me," he said. She didn't say anything, and her arm still covered her eyes. Her mouth was straight. He lifted himself up and touched her arm. "I was sort of lost in the plants, and I just happened to—"

"I've never liked the word," she said, sitting up. "Are you ready to go inside?"

"That's fine, but answer some of the questions, please."

"Let's come up with some other word for it," she said. "'Kidnapped' sounds so melodramatic."

"What if I were to kidnap you?"

"You bring a little something different to it. Something cozy, more like children cuddling up to sleep in the daytime."

"Yeah, it could even be something like dozing off on the plane ride back to Florida together."

"Not Florida. What about San Francisco?"

"Sure, New York even."

"Or you have a home, right?"

"Yeah, I have a home where I live."

"Let's go inside," she said. "I think I'm burning."

His room was a dark box without windows, and the cardinal lamp didn't do anything except look strange to their eyes. They were used to the sunshine. He sat down on the bed in the stream of the fan, and it blew on all the sun in his skin. The television station had come back, and the morning news was on without volume. He watched it, thinking. Honey patted her swimsuit cups. "They're pretty dry," she said, and she slipped her muumuu on, covering herself up.

Kyle stood up from the bed and went to the dresser. In the mirror, she watched herself twist her hair into a wet bun. She tied the clumps into a hanging ball on the back of her head and dug in her purse again, bringing out her tin of lip dew. She took off the cap and rubbed the dew on her lips. She sucked on her lips and rubbed them together. They looked greasy and slick, and Kyle smelled strawberries. He opened the top drawer and went through the things inside. "I have a nice pair of sunglasses that I found. Do you wear sunglasses?"

"I'm not really good at accessories."

"Just cosmetics."

"You mean lip dew?"

He pulled the designer glasses out of the drawer and unfolded the ear blades in the lamplight. The tortoiseshell lit up, and all the specks went on fire, and the gold plate burned and reproduced the skull of bulb inside the shade. The lenses sent their shapes down as dirty eclipse light on the wood of the dresser, and Honey picked them up and wore them in front of the mirror. He got close enough to see her eyes. They were muddy orbs, the color of river water through the amber tint, and he felt wiggles come into her hips. She broke away toward the mirror, and her music video poses were dead-on physicalities of the wicked and fresh. She danced. He swayed behind her, watching her moves.

Leaf gutters funneled rain through the strata of flapping green chutes. Gnarled branches streamed backwards up the hill, away from the gray deluge and into the terrestrial walls of black torch and saw palmetto. Banana tree leaves bobbed and nodded, and botanical bayonets rattled in the wind. Hitting rain beat the waxed foliage like a drum choir climax, and nested bowls of pink blossoms tilted full of water. Roadside donkeys stopped strolling to suck the twigs. Kyle watched them from the back bench of an open-sided safari taxi, and drips fell from the yellow awning like automatic rounds. Just he and the driver sat there in the storm with rows of empty bench seats between them. The driver turned around with an arm over the back of his seat. "Neddies drinking off the trees, eh?"

"Beasts of ease."

The road was open ahead, free of the forested narrows, and light showed the columns of silver showers falling. The collected dealings glided across the surface of the asphalt with drops breaking and speaking like an upset crowd. Behind the truck was a dark alley of road edged by neon brambles. Kyle had her keys in his hand. A gold whistle hung from the ring, and he put it in his mouth and blew. His air shot through the metal tube without resistance, and no sound came out. He dropped the dummy whistle and rattled the set. It was like a metal teething ring. Something made him want to bite the keys. He sat there deranged-legged, and his foot sputtered on the floorboards waiting for the rain to stop. A voice came blaring in on the radio. The cabman picked up the receiver and said a line of words with his thumb on the button and the coiled rubber wire bouncing in front of the rain-beaten windshield. He turned back to Kyle. "Sorry, got another fare. Maybe it'll stop soon."

"That's alright," Kyle said, and he stepped out into the rain, and the donkeys in the ditch turned to look at him with the rain hitting them all over and causing their lids to envelope their brown, marble eyes. The safari truck moved through the water standing in the road. Red raindrops fell through the color of the taillights, and the truck curved out of sight around the bend in the rain. He walked under the leaves, and they spit and sprayed down splatters of water. The sun turned up while he was on the path. Butterscotch discs stuck to the canopy and drooled down melted light all over the branches. Then the sun disappeared behind another cloud leaving evaporated syrup in the heated wet air.

A figure stood on the Bronco.

The sky sucked up the fallen water and reclaimed it in platinum streaks. Quick peeks of sunbeam came down through the leaden clouds of haze that developed in the parking lot. Kyle walked across the gravel, studying the figure that blended slender with the fog. He was sticky and wet, and his sinuses were filled with humidity, and looking through the saturation, his eyes blurred. It was a heron. It stood on the hood swiveling its head from side to side. Kyle slowed down. The bird was as tall as a boy, but its curved tube of neck made it look hunched like an old man. Kyle inched close enough to see the velvet plumes that ran from its eye across its crown and out into the space behind its head like a streak of calligraphy across oriental woodblocks of the floating world. The heron got nervous. Its rusted red thigh drew its leg akimbo, and a knee came out of the stick leg. It put its tined foot down again at the base of the Bronco windshield. Kyle moved closer, rolling his feet not to shift the gravel and scare the bird. The heron put another foot on the sloped glass and tried to walk up the windshield. It got hung in the black mechanisms of the wiper, and the blade lifted. The heron's loose throat started a hoarse croak. The wiper snapped back into place, and the heron walked on top of the roof, croaking and stepping over the bars of the luggage rack. Kyle inched closer, and to his right, all the white caught his eye. He froze in the parking lot. In the aluminum jon boat, Zataurus stirred from sleep with his jacket covering his upper body like a blanket. The heron flapped its wings and hopped but didn't fly. It calmed down and stood there. Zataurus stirred and made small noises. He lifted himself up and propped himself on one arm, rubbing his eye. He rubbed his head and looked at Kyle. He looked at the heron standing on the roof of the Bronco he guarded. Zataurus stood up.

He walked forward, putting his jacket on, wrapping it around himself and finding the silk-lined arm hole without taking his eyes off Kyle. He jerked the jacket onto his shoulders, tucked his bottom lip under his teeth and whistled. In the cabin of the cruiser, there was motion, and Diamondy came out onto the back deck. He yelled inside to the others and then jumped the gunwale, landing on the dock and running. "My name's Kyle." Zataurus didn't say anything. He walked fast and straight. Kyle took a step backwards. "I'm just here to pick up the truck," he said, and he held up her keys. Zataurus's eyes were fixed on his face, unbreaking. He walked forward. His face was serious. Kyle dropped the keys into the gravel. He turned, and running came over him, and he sprinted through the cars. He heard foot crunches in the gravel behind him, but he didn't look back. He just ran. Movement dragged on the dark hoarse croak of the great blue heron. It was spooked enough to fly, too, and under a tin shelter, a stagnant crowd of people bobbed and dragged their feet across the pavement like a hexed herd. They boarded the interisland passenger ferry, and Kyle ducked in among them, battling through and excusing himself, body-checking bellies and elbowing handbags. He prayed for mythological athleticism, wings of speed that could wisp his form into oily streaks of crayon color.

He ran on his toes trying not to get ahead of his own body and windmill headlong into the gravel. He jumped down a bank into a freshet ditch where the rainwater filtered off the land. In the park, bullate leaves slapped him wet across the face, and fungal growths clutched the trees like fan-shaped sacks of jelly. Imported geese cocked their necks and wore battle wings to fight the children that fed them, and their orange beaks climbed into bumps on their foreheads like outbreaks of sumac. Kyle ran through causing flaps and honks, and the fountain in the middle of the pond jetted a ring of mist into the air. Osiers of the willow dragged the surface of the water and concealed people sitting on the grassy bank. Kyle parted the curtain of limp branches and pivoted to avoid a hand planted in the grass. In the open field, he lockstepped with boys playing soccer with a basketball, and their youth rode them across the field flawlessly and in formation. The emergency gave him a youth he didn't use all the time, and it coursed super fluids through his system. He was a higher-level runner in the crisis. The boys' legs blurred beside him, and the slick basketball rolled gripless across the damp field of grass, the air inside ringing with kicks.

Downtown was crowded. People surrounded him, but he also felt a vacancy, like he wasn't being chased anymore. He slowed to a fast walk in the foot traffic, weaving through the lanes of people, and a salesman honed in on him, talking a fast patter. His fingers braided palm fronds into hats, masks, statues and baskets while he talked, and the newly woven items were as green as when they still grew on the tree. The older ones sat brittle and drained of chlorophyll on the table. The palm mask had a rubber band attached. The salesman saw Kyle looking at it, and he gave it interest, too. He modeled it for Kyle, and his brown eyes showed through the crooked holes. There was a sea turtle made out of palms. The salesman lifted the shell off and demonstrated the basket area by sticking his fist down inside the turtle. "To hold things, jewelry or anything coming out of your pockets," he said. Kyle had planned to bring souvenirs back for his family. He pulled cash out of his canvas wallet and bought a lidded sea turtle basket, choosing the model that had already been shown to him, fresh and green. It was for his mother. The bells rang in the church behind him, and the salesman wrapped the sea turtle in newspaper pages. Kyle watched him, thinking the sea turtle carries its home on its back, and the sea turtle is a homebody, and the sea turtle is always naked around the house. The salesman lowered the bundle carefully into a hot pink shoebox. He covered it with the lid and thumbed a little dirge beat on top. "I'm sad to let this one go," the salesman said. Kyle looked around, scanning the crowd while he talked. "I had a bond with this one for some reason. That must mean you got a good eye. Don't tell nobody, but that's the best one I made all month, and that's the truth. That one'll hold water," the salesman said.

His white suit showed through the tinted windows. The Bronco stopped at a pedestrian crosswalk. People straggled and called after one another, shopping and strolling through the narrow streets and sunny facades of the pastel village.

The Catholic church was dark and cool. In the narthex, a seashell stoup was carved out of the stone wall, and Kyle let his hands fall into the clear holy water. He stared at his pale palms underwater and then cupped the liquid up over his bowed head, blessing himself and asking for a dosage of clear thought to idle his vital signs. His heart beat fast, and his breath rippled the surface of the little pool. Drips ran off his fingers, and water falling back to itself echoed off the stone walls. Holy water soaked into the gummy strands of twine that his hair had become from swimming in saltwater and sprinting through mugginess. Families filed in and grew solemn at the threshold. Low organ notes whispered air through gold flues that hung like pan-pipes on the far wall of the sanctuary, and he watched the acolytes getting ready for the service. Their robes swallowed them. Waiting to line up behind the banner bearers, they straddled their long candle lighters like broomstick horses and played with the extenders so the wax-coated tapers came out and retracted again. A man in plain clothes lit the wicks with a cigarette lighter, and the sacred service flame grew strong. Kyle and his sister had been acolytes for his grandfather's funeral. He followed a family of blonds down the aisle and sat across from them, the boys with spheres of living curls and silk knots at their throats. In the rack at his knees, literature leaned forward, and a leather loop strapped a golf pencil to the binding of a guestbook.

The service began, and the acolyte flames transferred to brass-capped candlesticks on the communion table. Exposed bread sat plated on the white cloth next to gold-lidded trays, stacked like a futuristic parking deck, and Kyle imagined the tiny cups inside. He always wanted more grape juice than the glasses held, more transfigured gore, and shimmering swaths sewed to the gonfalons trilled the milk and honey light like fabric luminaries, puckered and dimpled on brazen stands. Looking up in the cool sanctuary, the soaring beams came together in a hanging finial at the ceiling peak. Electrical wires slalomed through the links of long chandelier chains, the fixtures hanging still at the end, hexagonal tubes of creamy panes set in wrought iron garnishments. Sunlight barely made it through the stained window, and it came through suspiring Christ, terrified in the garden, his body crumpled in his robe and emblazoned sash, begging not to, and his palms faced each other so no balls of egoic energy escaped his body towards heaven. Only humility floated up like a feather pulled by reverse gravity, and Christ looked into the cobalt expanse of glass above his head, his doughy eyes tan with earthliness and expressing medieval sadness, congenital melancholy for the words of every biography that burned in the sky. He was hemmed in by doves in beveled boxes. The jeweled cup floated and overflowed.

A woman in a black dress sat down in front of him, her body a curved canister inside stretched fabric, and she held a child straddling her shape. The boy kicked movement at her ridge of panty line with a tiny little saddle oxford, and a multicolored train barreled across the elastic bands of his socks. His cherubic leg swung doughy and mottled purple in the cool sanctuary, and an older couple sat down with the mother and child. Kyle studied the backs of their necks and heads. He sought refuge, and the priest processed from the chancel, turning through wooden gates in the altar rails, and he was a rotund black man with ochre skin and auburn hair shaped up into a box. His loud stole came from Mozambique when he was on a mission trip there, he said, and the tribal deer were stitched leaping in appreciation. He read scripture to the congregation, and Kyle followed along in the pew Bible. Only the red words were important, he used to think. Platitudes that slid through other mouths were typeset in black, but his were written in red on the thin pages sent down through the ages to them in the wooden pews, and after hearing the words, he didn't know whether he heard them with his ears or the sentiments transcended language. The polyglots of religious feeling talked in soothing murmurs that the rational mind didn't understand, and the dye was hard to see looking at the cut edge of one tissue page. Kyle closed the book, stacking the onion skins together, and the edge collected with color. He felt power in his hands, and waves of worship washed over him. Water collected in his eyes. He had to look up to the flying buttresses, invoking the scientific spirits, gravity and surface tension, to keep the water from spilling over the palpebral pink rims of his eyes and streak down his cheeks. Tears clung to his lashes, and the eye hair was soaked and spiked. He had the same problem at his grandfather's funeral.

The imago talked about love, "Flesh love in the back rooms and love in the fingertips and love pounding in the heart and hurting. A love so painful no acetaminophen can touch it, a bloodless love carried out in secret, gestured unnoticed, familiar love like the touch of a blanket you've been under all night. From the waist of the holy ghost, bright hulas ring, and from the waist of the holy ghost, comfortable clothes hang, and from the waist of the holy ghost, I cheer you up, my people." Slinging solace from the hip, the priest raised his arms in blessing, and the true voice of the paraclete issued forth from the black foam of the backhanded pulpit mic. The congregation stood up smiling, and a hymn of praise was raised to prepare for holy communion.

He went with the flow of people out of the church. The ensemble bands of green and silver faded down the panel of the Bronco door. Through the purple tinted windows, he saw them moving inside. Impastos of dried mud stuck to the fenders, and the postmodern crusts showed the truck's history of motion. The Bronco sat parallel parked at the bottom of the stone steps.

Tropical panoply locked behind the truck. The spotted glass of the window moved, and the door opened. Kyle's vision, looking out from the church steps, granulated in sick fear, and monarchs were born inside his stomach. Like with home film strips, periwinkle chemical damage spotted the edges of his sight. He was confused, and the aim jarred as in a great projector crash. Zataurus stepped out of the backseat, a chimera of man and wattage, sun lion and dream figure. He was a pinup for thuggish orphans, wearing so many heads and holding the rage of a beast pastiche in the noon spotlight. His gang flanked him under the canopy of his clout, and their attitudes jammed together in a row of magnified crow faces, chocked with attitude. They looked ready to piñata-beat the communion out of him, and their neon throwbacks itched to forehead kick. They jabbered at him, and their language was thick with island slurs. They berated him in a bunt-tongued mixture of old Dutch grunts and smoked-out ebonics, a bad lexicon of oceanic cusses, growled in a din he didn't get.

He stuck close to the family he had worshiped behind. The grandmother and grandfather walked side by side holding hands, and the mother held the child behind them. Kyle hung with them in their pack. The sidewalk disappeared, and they stretched into a single file line on the edge of the street. The cars passed close. He heard the drug runners whooping behind him, and he premeditated the feeling of them grabbing his shoulders and throwing him down from behind. He didn't want to wrestle or talk. They followed him, shouting things, and it sounded like strings of a stupid gibberish. It sounded like onomatopoeia. A cappella in the street, the mother still sang the parting hymn into her little boy's face, and their noses touched while they walked. The babe could fit his whole hand in his mouth, and he sucked on it, riding his mother's curves and watching the temporary construction fence blur by his big child eyes. She glossed over some lyrics and hummed parts and picked the words up again when she knew them. The famous chorus came around again, strong and pretty out of her mouth, and there was feeling in her song. The boy giggled and cooed in unison, splaying his wrists and wiggling in her arms. The grandparents turned into the fence gap, leaving the crowded street and walking through the empty construction site. Kyle followed, looking over his shoulder, and they walked on a mound of packed dirt. To either side, a blunge of rainwater, clay and sand mixed together and filled the ditches with calamine mud. The heavy equipment had cleated pillbox indentions across the mound they walked on, and the rain had filled in the squares. The puddles were capped with a mother-of-pearl film, and their weight squeezed a sizzle of bubbles out of the ground.

A forgotten Mountain Dew distilled in the sun like bottled absinthe in the backhoe's caged cabin. They ducked under a section of caution tape that bounced in the wind, and the grandfather pointed to the skeletal beams of the new structure and talked about the building methods. The side yard used to be a garden, and the ground had been trenched for the laying down of pipes. The disruption wound among the landscaped beds, and a shovel truck sat parked beside a koi water feature surrounded by flowering bushes.

Coming out to the street, all the blinkers flashed orange under the high meridian light, and the sedan doors whispered to unlatch. The grandfather held a keyless entry fob surreptitiously by his thigh, and he opened the back and front passenger-side doors for the women in his life. Kyle caught the young mother's glance when she turned to slide in across the pleated leather. They exchanged smiles, and she seemed to Kyle like a natural nurturer. She was a feminine protector, he thought, and her nature and face gave him cozy respite. Her kind eyes were big and brown like nests. Kyle moved down the sidewalk grinding grains of sand against the concrete underfoot. The rain had washed the mud out of the construction site and across the walkway where it baked dry. He walked on isles of grit that glittered like little littered stars in the sun. He looked over his shoulder.

The party at McDonald's was in the parking lot. Kyle steered toward people and kept near voices and witness eyes. A man in the parking lot wore a khaki suit, paisley tie and a furry pimp hat. He turned a flashlight on and off in the blinding daylight. He danced, trying to attract traffic to the jewelry sale set up in the tent behind him. Black rope chokers, silver ornaments and amethyst tokens were spread on the folding table, and the girl helping customers wore a tall mohawk. A fuzzy shadow grew on the flanking brown scalp.

Kyle walked into a colony of people. They stood in the grass under the marquee and golden arches. Out of the back of a caravan, video equipment played an animated movie. Kyle blended in, grimacing to squint through the bright heat, watching the cartoon through inconstant gaps in the swaying shoulders in front of him. Everyone ate lunch standing and watching the screen that showed an animated catbird, drunk on wine. Out of its black nib, it babbled a different language, and the crowd read the dialogue that scanned across the screen in yellow subtitles. They found out the catbird was on a quest to look for more wine. Agreement and understanding elbowed through the people, and the catbird stumbled at the brink of a concrete bath, whistling drinking songs at the edge of the dry basin stained with a claret residue. A cartoon housewife came out of the cottage. She uncorked a bottle and let its contents gasp into the bath and went inside again. The catbird beak-drank the wine and fluttered its gray wings against its songbird belly, happy, the caption said, "Lark-like," and the avian wino was funny and likeable. Kyle walked through the laughing crowd. He overheard someone say the cartoon was from Haiti.

More people sat against the wall of McDonald's picnicking on the fast food. Their waxed yellow wrappers served as lap plates. They flattened their to-go bags like placemats in the eave shade, and one boy ate lunch on an empty newspaper box. His swinging legs gonged the metal side, and there was break dancing around the corner on a big swatch of kitchen linoleum laid out on the sidewalk. Keyboard beats, recorded on a mixed cassette, came out of a car stereo, and young people stood on the trunk watching the dance. Different breakers took the linoleum, and it hosted spinning backs and rotating shorts. The maneuvers were acrobatic. Freezes halted the motion in stylish poses, and the best of them stood rotating on his head with his arms out to the side like an inverted cross.

Inside the restaurant, a mass of people formed unclear lines at the stainless steel counter, most of them in Sunday church dress, shoulder pads and hot-splotched ties. The menu glowed. Backlit photos of perfect sandwiches tilted down at them. Kyle walked toward the people standing farthest from the counter where he thought the end of the line must be, and he passed a pair of men in conversation. One of them wore a polo under a cotton T-shirt that featured a digital image of himself with his arm around an elderly woman. "Happy Mother's Day '97," the mauve caption across his stomach read. He listened to the men, and the one who did most of the talking carved the air with his hands. Kyle got to the counter and ordered from the dollar menu. A small female employee pressed her fingers into the worn plastic pad of the register.

"You don't want the value meal?" she said.

"I think it's cheaper this way."

"With the value meal, you get a bigger fry and drink, though."

"This is good the way you have it rung up now," he said.

McDonald's used to hand out honey in little tubs. The bee drawn on the foil flap used to go down on a white blossom, and there was a collage of nature. The empty cells of the comb decorated the background like complex latticework, and he wondered as a little boy whether the bee was robbed for the tub, or it gave of itself willingly. The flower throat hid its face, so the flap's artist gave it no expression. Drawn dancing on the petal tongues, that intoxicated, obsessive creature knew the way to the meadows. Kyle would eat in cartoon underwear, and if the channel needed changing, he had to stand on the player piano to press the buttons on the television and then twist the dial to move the rotary antenna outside. McDonald's must have carried honey for their nuggets, but he always used them on the fries. The sugar and salt mixed on the stick of potato, burned yellow, and the honey strings stretched into drips that fell like thick blond ropes back to the tub. There was an art to spinning the fry and spooling the gold gloss long enough to draw the fry across his lap. Memories were fat and sweet, and they stopped carrying honey tubs a long time ago on the mainland, but he asked again, thinking the island franchises might be different. The girl behind the counter shook her head, and he walked toward the condiment stand with his bag. He never switched to ketchup, but he needed napkins. He felt a forearm in the small of his back and lips at his ear, and he was pinned against the condiment stand in the middle of the McDonald's crowd.

"Where's Honey?" Diamondy whispered.

"I don't know."

"You had her keys," he said.

"She asked me to do her a favor. I was just helping her."

"Where?"

"I don't know."

"But where is she?"

"I don't know."

"Where is she now?" Diamondy whispered, singsong.

"I don't know."

"Where was she when she asked the favor?" He pushed in harder at the small of his back. The edge of the condiment counter dug into his stomach. "Where was she when you got her keys from her? Right now it's just her deal, but you're making everybody feel rabid as hell, so say you're story. You ought to."

"I work at the Hidden Harbor Resort. She was there and needed her truck. I volunteered to help. I didn't know it was your truck. I thought it was hers. She had the keys, and I didn't mean to make anybody mad."

"Alright, you finally did good now." The forearm pressure pulled out of his lumbar. "So bro, you just enjoy your value meal," he said. Kyle stood up and turned around. He watched Diamondy make his way through the crowded restaurant and out the double glass doors into the parking lot. The Bronco eased through with its back hatch open. Diamondy stepped on the bumper and jumped in through the opening. The truck never stopped rolling, and it sped up with him inside. Kyle touched his neck and rubbed a tickled feeling out of his skin. He imagined a few black mustache hairs must have grazed his neck. He felt shaky. He thought about food, and he wanted to eat. He lifted his drink cup and bag and pink shoebox from the condiment counter. He walked one way. He turned around and walked the other way like a toy car bumping and going. Being told to eat by Diamondy made part of him not want to. He stopped and looked at the design printed on the to-go bag. Blue made him thirsty. Red and yellow made him hungry. Solid fields disbanded into geometric patterns of dots, and the optical illusion did more to confuse him.

Across the street at the convenient store, symbols and declarations were carved into the black phone booth paint, and Kyle lifted the blue receiver from its silvery hook.

"Hidden Harbor Resort, this is Marie. How may I help you?"

"Maria, it's Kyle on the ground crew. Is Manny working today?"

"Oh, hey, Kyle. Can you hold on just a second please?"

"It's an emergency. I need to speak with him. Is he out there?"

The hold music came on, Debussy. Kyle stood listening to it with his head bowed into the booth trying to block out all the sound coming from the convenient store.

"Manny here."

"Manny, it's Kyle. There's some trouble with the girl from last night. There are some guys who are mad at her and mad at me. They're in a Bronco."

"Not Zataurus?"

"Yes, and I had to tell them Honey was at the hotel, and they're probably headed there now looking for her. Could you do me a favor and warn Honey? Just please tell her to stay in my room and hide there and not come out."

"I can do that for you. You alright?"

"Just a little nervous. And if they pull up there asking questions, I don't know, do whatever you think."

"Throw them off the trail somehow?"

"Yeah, or whatever. But be safe. I'm not asking you to stick your neck out unnecessarily."

"I can do a little song and dance maybe. Hell, I'm already dressed like an organ grinder monkey."

In the packed sand, he ate his french fries first. Pinching the golden potato blades and bringing them into his mouth, he leaned back against a palm trunk behind the dumpster and bushes of the restaurant back. A motorcycle roared in the drive-thru lane. He pushed his shoe heels across the packed white sand trying to get comfortable. His spine rocked against the tree, and he ate the lunch, too nervous to taste anything. Wind blew through the fronds up over his head, and he listened to the rattle with devotion and attention. He listened for anything. He listened for words to come into his ears that meant something. He wanted to catch a schizophrenia that could withdraw him from reality. The pink shoebox sat in the sand beside him. He finished the squashed cheeseburger and chewed away the soft cheese melted to the wrapper. He wadded the bag with all the trash collected inside. He stood up and punted it into the bushes. He paced in the patch of sand, kicking at it and stomping. He kicked a AA battery twice, and it barreled and spun out. He picked it up and threw it towards the McDonald's roof. He listened but never heard it hit anything. Then he circled the pink shoebox looking down at the white lines and the futura font. He thought high heels had come in the box maybe. He thought of home. His mother never wore high heels. She wore Sam & Libby's with leather bows. Then he knelt down and uncovered the lid. He looked at the sea turtle basket woven out of palm fronds. In the palm tree above, real palm fronds grew. He looked up at them and couldn't believe they could ever be crafted into a sea turtle basket like he had in the shoebox on the ground. He was impressed with the gift he would give. He had just seen a sea turtle living in the harbor water, so the souvenir could go with his story and mean a little more. The real sea turtle couldn't look like palm fronds. High heels didn't look like baskets, he thought.

He crossed the street again and went to the pay phone. He reversed the charges with the operator and listened to it ring with the blue receiver against his face and all the holes of the mouthpiece at his lips. It picked up his breathing and reproduced it in his ear, and he blew a stream of test breath, loud and hard. It distorted, and he heard it in the earpiece, and then the ringing stopped, and there was a series of clicks.

"Hello? Kyle?"

"Hey, Mom."

"Hey, it's my blue-eyed baby boy in the middle of the blue ocean," she said. "Kyle's on the phone. Do you want to pick it up in the bedroom," she yelled away from the phone. "Your father's in the basement with your sister's new deer."

"A deer? A real deer?"

"I'm afraid so. She brought it home from the vet clinic. It has white spots and a strange pattern on its face like a white mask. It can barely walk. She's at work now, but we've been having to feed it with a bottle every few hours, but what's going on with you? You've decided to come home?"

"Well, yeah, maybe."

"Oh really? Why?"

"There's a little bit of trouble."

"Okay, alright, what's happening?"

"I'm at a convenient store pay phone, and these guys have sort of been chasing me."

"Oh why Kyle?"

"They're drug dealers is what I've heard, and they're involved with this girl that I've met."

"And you got caught with her?"

"Not with her, but they can't find her, and she's in my room back at the hotel."

"Kyle, what color?"

"They're black, but she's white."

"Okay, what are we going to do?" she said.

The bedroom phone clicked live. "Hello."

"Hey, Dad."

"Hey, how are you? It sure is good to hear your voice."

"Not too good really."

"What's the matter?"

"He's found a girl who's mixed up with drug runners. She's in his room at the hotel, and they're after him and her," his mother said.

"And they've been following me around town today," Kyle said. "It's my theory that drug dealers down here are like this generation's pirates."

"What are we going to do?" she said.

"I don't know. I called Manny, the bellhop, at the hotel and asked him to warn her."

"Well, I guess we need to get on the next plane to the Caribbean," his father said.

"No, no, no, no, no," Kyle said. "Yall don't have to do that."

"Or should he hang up with us and call the police?" his mother said. "Oh Kyle, oh Kyle. I just don't know."

"Okay, try to stay calm. Can you just get to the airport?" his father said. "Where are you now? Do you think you could get to the airport?"

"I could get a taxi, but I have things in my room, and the girl is in my room now, kind of hiding out. I should do something about that first, right?"

"Not by yourself. It's dumb to be a hero. Don't you want to call the police?" his mother said.

"I'd like to just calm things down and try to stay here without any trouble," Kyle said. "I'm having a good time. It's just being chased by drug dealers that's off-putting."

"We can come down there," his father said.

"What good would we do against drug dealers?" his mother said.

"No, yall don't need to do that."

"Kyle, we will if you want us to."

"I can handle it. I'm just going to walk back toward the hotel leisurely, take my time on the back roads, maybe even swim in through the harbor."

"Drowning would also be bad," his father said.

"I'm a strong swimmer."

"You never know."

"I'm just going to see what's going on and what needs to happen next. I don't know if you'd consider this a big deal or not. Really, technically, nothing has happened."

"Well, it's a big deal to us," she said.

"Alright, I mainly just called to think out loud with somebody. Thanks, guys. I'm going to get moving now."

"You're going back to the hotel?"

"I need to, yeah. I can't just fly away and leave everything. That's the first step, I think, just to go back to the hotel and see what's happening. Maybe nothing is even going on."

"Well, be careful, Kyle, and there's nothing wrong with calling the police. It's better to be safe than sorry," she said. "No stupid girl is worth it."

"Be careful, buddy," he said.

"I will."

"And call us when you get back to the hotel, alright?"

"I will."

"We love you so, so much."

"I love you, too."

"And be so careful."

"I will."

"Call us when you get there, okay? And if you can think of anything we can do from here, call us again, or if we need to come down there, we will."

"Okay, thanks."

"Do you want us to call the hotel and ask if anything's happened, so you'll know whether you can go back or not?"

"No, that would be strange to ask. How would you ask that?"

"I don't know," his mother said. "It's better to be strange than dead."

"I'm not going to be dead or strange. Nothing's going to happen. I'll be fine. I need to go. I don't like being out in the open like this. I'm in the middle of a convenient store parking lot."

"Alright, we love you. Call us."

"I love you, buddy," he said.

"I love you, too," Kyle said. "I will. Alright."

"Alright. Bye."

"Bye," Kyle said.

"Bye."

He walked on the edge of another storm. Raindrops smacked in the bushes beside the road. Two big drops fell on his arm, but that was all. The wind rearranged his hair. He combed it with his fingers, and the wind blew through it again. He brushed it out of his eyes, and the wind kept blowing, and his curls whipped him in the face. He let the wind do whatever it wanted to do with his hair, and he had never been to a barber. He had never had a professional haircut. His grandmother had always cut his hair, leaving his ducktail instead of cutting straight across the back. The wind styled it now, and the wind had wild taste. Leaves bounced and jammed and shook like waving hands, their pale undersides in and out of view. A wet pavement smell blew in from a distance, and the storms were periwinkle behind the flaring green banks of brush in the distance.

He walked under the trees beside a narrow road that led up the mountain's vertebrae. He climbed higher and saw a parade of storm clouds riding in off the sea like racecars on the high wind. Pewter undercarriages rode over his face, and the surface of the water rushed in on the drag. The sea was pocked with shadows and dappled with intermittent sunlight that came down through skylights in the clouds. Everything was being sucked in toward the island, like a hinterland magnet pulled the elements and the broken ceiling of cloud cover. The shapes contorted. Hooks and feathers and question marks curled in the swirling bodies above, and he walked through the parking lot for the public beach below, and it looked different in the daytime. The whitewashed arch was glaring in the sun and lavender when a cloud passed over. The other islands across the channel were closer and bigger than he thought they were. A family of seagulls balanced on the curved plaster wall that led down to the water. Some of them jumped into the wind and hovered on it when he walked by, and they honked in the air, back and forth, playing call and response through the keratin woodwinds that grew from their faces.

Her arm slept behind her in his bed. The room was dark, and the box fan blew. Kyle stepped on the heel of his shoe and slid it off without untying the knot, and with his bare foot, he stepped on the back of his other shoe. He kicked them both to the wall, and sand and gravel rumbled inside. His feet and legs were wet up to his knees. His cutoffs were damp, and the hanging threads stuck to his legs. Trash stuck to his feet, and his arches ached. He stretched them flat on the felt floor and wiped his legs dry with a towel. He eased himself onto the bed lying on top of the covers next to her. Her hair was feral and covering her face, and her arm twisted behind her back. It looked broken. He wasn't sleepy. He lay on his back staring up at the ceiling, and he laced his fingers together on top of his sternum. The change in his pocket shifted. It slid out of his pocket, most of it landing in Honey's unconscious palm. She came out of her nap, feeling the metal money. A noise came out of her mouth without her controlling it, and her fingers curled around the coins. She lifted herself up and sat leaning against the wall, pushing the twisted ropes of long, blond hair out of her face. She had put on one of his shirts, and it swallowed her. Her lips were puffed and hot. Her face was pink. A crease ran across her temple and cheek, and she gave caveman study to the money in her hand, staring at it and not recognizing it. Her face was asymmetrical and swollen. She laughed a slow sleep laugh and looked up at Kyle. "I never woke up with money in my hand before," she said.

"That's a good sign."

She lay down with her chin on his chest, and he put his arms around her. "Anytime there's something stressful going on, I automatically fall asleep," she said.

"I think I have to fly out tomorrow morning," he said. "I think you should come, too."

He slipped out from underneath her and rolled off the bed. He crouched down and pulled a navy suitcase out from under the metal bed frame.

"I didn't think this would ever happen," she said. "But in all honesty, I think they hid things from me, and as long as I was doing what they wanted me to, I was left out of anything sordid. I was stupid. I'm sorry."

"I'm a lot dumber than you are," Kyle said. He unzipped his suitcase around three sides of the rectangle and opened the flap. He dragged it over to the dresser and transferred his socks from the bottom drawer. Blunt beating came through the metal door. They stopped talking and froze, and the beatings happened again, muffled through the metal. "It's Manny," sounded like a stage whisper through the door, and Kyle unlocked the door and cracked it open. The white bar of burning outside blinded him, and he didn't see anything, but he smelled cigarette smoke.

"It's me," Manny said, and he pushed the door open more. A cigarette balanced between his fingers. The paper and dried leaves dissolved and became strings of blue smoke that streamed away from the ashy tip, like ghosts that floated toward the bathhouse where they disappeared, bridging the being worlds and going to the other side. Manny inhaled on the filter, and Kyle looked into his solid eyes. The squat drum of his bellboy hat sat crooked on his head, and the chin strap parted his grizzled beard. "Maunar saw you wading in through the mangroves carrying your shoes and a pink shoebox. She thought that was a strange combination and wanted me to come check on you."

Kyle nodded. "I'm alright."

"That's good to hear. We got three of them still hanging around here. One at the beach bar reading the newspaper, sometimes talking on a cell phone and drinking a ton of rum. Two more out front are throwing a little blue racquetball back and forth to each other. I threw it with them a little bit to get on their good sides. We triangled up right out there under the porte-cochere."

"What happened with the others? What about Zataurus?" Kyle said.

"They walked around the whole hotel and then drove away again in the Bronco."

"Listen, Manny, I think we have to get out of here, like off the island," Kyle said.

"Yeah, yeah, I've got some ideas right here," Manny said, tapping the rope-lined breast pocket of his uniform. "The exercise room on the third floor of the main building closes at nine tonight. At five after, I'll open those doors at the other end of the alley. They lead into the kitchen, and we can take the service elevator and grab some leftovers on the way up if you want. Sound good?"

"Five after?"

"Five after," Manny said. He held out his fist, and Kyle hammered down on top of it.

"Thanks, Manny."

Manny winked and turned around. He flicked his cigarette butt onto the roof of the bathhouse and strolled around the corner whistling with his hands in his pockets and his long hair hanging down the back of his burgundy bellhop jacket. Kyle closed the door, and Honey was on her knees at his suitcase. She worked on the second drawer from the bottom, pulling his shorts and cutoffs out, trailing ravels across the edge of the sliding box and restacking them in the bed of the rolling suitcase. "I don't have any of my own clothes to pack," she said.

"You can borrow that shirt you're wearing."

"Do you regret knowing me?" she said.

"I wish we had run into each other back in Florida somehow," he said.

"Me, too, Kaleidoscope. Me, too. Has anybody ever called you that before? As a nickname or anything?"

"Not to my face," he said.

She held up the shimmering green swimsuit and studied the black electrical tape that covered the orange hologram. She scratched at the corner with her fingernails. The tape peeled off. She wadded it into a ball and threw it at his chest. It hit him and fell to the floor rolling across the red felt. She folded the shimmering shorts twice, put them in the suitcase and pressed down, leaning on the whole stack to compress it.

"It looks like you're trying to resuscitate those clothes," he said.

"I don't even know how to do that."

"How many times have you pressed down?"

"Just twice."

"You would press down thirteen more times and then check for a pulse if those clothes were a dead person."

"What about that stuff on the desk?" she said. "Is that supposed to fit in here?"

He moved the brick bookends away from his books, and they stayed standing vertical without support. He made a flat stack of the books on the desk edge. The pictures of his family he slid toward the nail heads in the pine paneling. The chads reversed. The exit wounds changed to the blank white sides, and the puncture holes in the paper got a little bigger taking them off. He leaned over and picked up the other picture. It was facedown against the baseboards in the corner. He looked at Julie's face. He searched it for familiarity, wiped the dust off the glossy finish and slid it in with his family pictures. The whole stack he stuck into the middle pages of the new book on fishing Caribbean waters. He hadn't had a chance to rent a rod and reel yet. He flipped through the book, and a black and white figure drawing of a hook and half hitch caught his eye. He unplugged the lamp and wrapped the cord around the base. He got down on his knees beside Honey and lowered the things into the suitcase. He leaned over and kissed her on the corner of her mouth. The lamp was awkward, but she used spatial skills and rearranged the books so they made sense and fit with the other things she had already packed.

They kept the dimmer down in the exercise room. The wall sconces had been converted to electricity sixty years before, so white metal shafts took the place of wax sticks, and a low orange glow coated the looping filaments inside the flame-shaped bulbs. Diodes on the fitness equipment gave more visibility to the room. The treadmill consoles were personal scoreboards of beaded light. Red, yellow and green grids cycled through sample inclines and cardio glows, and the panels were like starship dashboards in a row across the room, blinking away in periodic deaths and pulsing again, glass scorpion hearts encased in plastic shadowboxes. Foam padded the rails. The line of treadmills looked like robot chariots, and in the corner by the ceiling, the mounted television screen was a blinded field, bending the room outward like a wide-angle lens, so the displays looked like city lights seen from a promontory. Rolled towels sat ricked against the wall. The blinds were drawn to the hall door, and slats lay slapped flat over windows that would have looked out at the night beach.

"They should be here soon," Manny said. He sat on the seat of an indoor rower drinking beer from a bottle. Don used his swipe card to get in, and Maunar followed him carrying a clasped laptop that hummed in her arms. The hall lights shone on their faces. Honey and Kyle sat together on the overturned suitcase, leaning against the textured wallpaper. "What did I tell you? I prepare you all the time," Manny said. Maunar plugged the laptop into the wall and connected it to the power source and the hotel network. It rested on the padded bench of the weight machine, and they gathered around, staring at the screen. The hotel's shield emblem was centered as the desktop background, and Manny came over taking a navy bandanna out of his back pocket. He tied it around his forehead so a triangle of folded corners stuck up straight in the air. "This is my lucky bandanna," he said.

"Why is it lucky?"

"My ex-wife bought it for me the night we met," he said. "Aw man, I changed out of my uniform. The plans I drew up were in the breast pocket."

"I don't think we'll need them. The plan is pretty simple."

Maunar's long fingers tapped at the keypad sounding like smacking animals, and white and blue websites flashed through the monitor. They queried for an early morning flight to Atlanta, but the search came up empty. Everything early to Orlando and Miami and Fort Lauderdale was full, too.

"You can't smoke in here, can you?" Manny said.

"It's an exercise room."

"But nobody's exercising."

"Yes, I am," Maunar said. "Exercising my right to breathe clean air."

"You really know how to burn me, little girlfriend."

Don stood and paced around with his hands clasped on top of his head, his row of fingers sinking into his spongy dome of hair. "Try another city," he said. "And get rid of that lucky bandanna." Maunar tracked her fingertip along the touchpad, and the cursor responded, darting across the screen. Don paced up onto the belt of one of the still treadmills and gripped the padded rails on either side of the console panel.

"Here's a six a.m. for New Orleans," Maunar said.

Honey looked at the screen and squinted at the bright display. A column of advertisements ran the length of the monitor to the right of the flight information. An ad was in motion. The streamers glistened, and the digital ribbons of purple and green laced through the eyes of drama masks and feather-laced tiaras, and a clarinet and trombone came rotating into view out of the yellow background as if they were floating in an anti-gravity chamber. Honey read the words that flashed on the screen. "Laissez les bon temps rouler," she said. She scrunched her nose, and sparkles took over the capital letters, and they disappeared into the darkest hues of the gouraud shading. She looked at Kyle.

"Let the good times roll," he said.

"Now you're talking. Book it," Manny said. He leaned over and tapped the screen over the hyperlink with his middle fingernail. Liquid crystals shone through his amber beer bottle and clarified the little bit left sloshing inside. "I got people there I can put you in touch with."

"It's not your trip, Manny. Guys, is that what you want to do?" Maunar said.

"I'll put it on my card," Kyle said. He pulled his canvas wallet out of his back pocket. Velcro made the flaps scratch apart, and he expanded the folds and pulled a card out of a clear plastic slot. Maunar entered information from the front. She turned the card over and entered more numbers and gave the card back to Kyle. The computer whirred and clicked inside to process the transaction. An exterior busy light pulsed on the body of the computer, and a little hourglass cartwheeled on the screen. "Your cursor's an hourglass," Kyle said. "That should be a new expression, like if you're confused and you need to think, you could say, 'Hold on. My cursor's an hourglass.'"

"You're sure about this?" Maunar said.

"Oh yeah," Kyle said.

The opposite wall was a dark mirror from ceiling to floor, and they were all in the reflection, an alternate exercise room, phantom people hypnotized by a white-blue light in front of them. Black equipment rods barred the reflection, and the scene looked like an experimental utopia where happiness expanded into unusual situations. He saw from the wall's perspective instead of his own, and the wall was out of his body. The wall was wiser and more complete than he was. It had been around longer, but it had only seen fitness people, nothing like the crew in the reflection then. He experienced something extra for a wave of time. Screen light was the new firelight. Except for the technology, their old huddle was an ancient one. The reflection in the mirror exhumed a mystery among them, and he saw it darkly in the room, and it already looked and felt like a memory to him even though he was there living it, and he was able to reminisce about the present and think back about the people who were right there next to him. Honey looked at Kyle, followed his eyes, and her face went full in the mirror, too. Don looked up. Maunar looked at the mirror, and Manny did, and one by one, they all stared forward with their ghost story faces lit from below by the computer light, and they held their poses for a split second to compose an ultrabaroque sitting of themselves. His mind stopped and locked the glass's spitted view of the characters, and the mirrored surface was an illusory threshold. Then they broke the pose and refocused on the computer, tilting at treadmills in the dark after-hours of the fitness room.

The blue rubber of the racquetball was worn down. Manny raised his hand, calling for it, and Slaw tossed it over. It was slick and smooth to the touch, and powdered concrete streaked the little sphere like comet scars. They had been bouncing it off the wall under the orange glow of the streetlight. Manny put his beer bottle down on a cobblestone, and the spangled grit in the mortar sparkled. He shuffled his feet and flicked the racquetball side-armed at the wall, and it shot back with weird spin like a superball in low bounces of different lengths across the uneven stones. Manny got down and crabbed sideways to field it with both hands, his necklaces dangling wild with his hair. "Lively little sucker," he said.

Manny threw it again, and adding geometry to the throw, he hit a spot high and left of dead in front of him, so the racquetball came hero-bounding back toward Slaw. He hunkered to evaluate it, frisking tall and closing in. He backpedaled and got up, and the puff-paint shirt rode his torso column. Manny saw a rack of his ribs, and a width of slack busted in the gap between his shorts and the elastic waistband of his striped boxers. He climbed an air ladder, looking up the length of his stretched arm, and the ball sailed over his fingertips. Clopping back to the drive with one foot then the other, he pivoted and flicked his ankles into a short-fire sprint after the ball that had trumped his jump. Manny framed his mouth with curved holler hands and funneled his voice after him, "You're a card, boy," and to Ralph in a normal volume, "Look at him go. He's something else, huh? I wish I could run like that."

"Whatever you say, he runs with a piano on his back."

"You're telling me you can run faster?"

"Much faster."

"Give yourself a high five, and all you're doing is clapping. Let's see it. Melt it."

Ralph took off after Slaw. His white pocket sacks were weighted full, and they came slinging out the bottom of his shorts banging against his long thighs. He caught up to Slaw at the edge of the circular jungle, the center of the driveway's roundabout. The racquetball disappeared through oars of leaves, and they stood at the arced curb looking and pointing into the verdant tangles of lush plant life. Manny faced the porte-cochere where his brown van was parked and waved for them to come out. In the lobby, Kyle saw the signal and pulled on the inside of Honey's arm. The sensor above the automatic doors noticed them, and Kyle lifted his suitcase by the handle so the wheels wouldn't chatter over section gaps in the concrete walkway. The side panel of the van jutted out and coasted rearwards on its track. Don ushered them inside and slammed the panel forward behind them.

Manny climbed into the driver's seat, wedging his beer in a trough of the plastic dash. He cranked the engine and pulled out from under the porte-cochere. The van pitched on its shocks to veer through the roundabout, and Manny stuck his head out the driver-side window. "Sorry about that, fellows," he said. He held his arm out at them in the increasing wind speed. Ralph lifted

95

a leaf that acted in his hand like a sheet of paper skewered on a stem. Slaw pointed into the wall of darkness through the firework tendrils of a spider lily's legs, wielding his cell phone unfolded as a flashlight.

Two fires burned where Manny camped. The van sat parked in its usual spot. Its front bumper nudged a tree trunk, and the headlights poured into the thick, doubling everything with shadows. Manny was confident with the fires he had built. He leaned inside the van, and the headlight beams left the woods. Light from the two new fires took over the campsite.

A ground fire matured on the trampled apron of dirt next to the van. Stones and conchs surrounded the charred ash pit, and Manny didn't chop his limbs. He just dragged sections into the fire, letting the ends dissolve like cigarettes, and the rest, he left sticking out in twisted radials like a witch's familiars come to feed on the flames. Maunar, Don, Kyle and Honey sat between the limbs on wool blankets, and champagne light gathered and attached to their faces. The rising heat column pumped the edge of a blue tarp that Manny set up. It bellied as an awning between two tent poles on one side, and it scrolled around the van's luggage rack on the other. Manny brought out the two bags of ice they had stopped for, and from under the tarp canopy, he looked at his fires and his guests. He nodded. "I don't have people over too often," he said. "This is nice, walking out and seeing yall sitting there like hobos." He laughed. He put the ice on the ground and took his shirt off, easing his necklaces through the neck hole and arranging the medallions and claws and teeth on his bare chest. "Anybody else feel free to rid yourself of clothing." He pitched his wadded shirt through the open van door. "Maunar? Honey? No?" He bent down to the cooler. Beer and a bag of Skittles floated in the old ice water. He took them out and dumped the cooler at the camp edge, washing the bushes, and he replaced the beer and bag of candy in the plastic liner with solid chips of fresh ice on top.

The second fire, a barrel fire, hollowed half the darkness with lapping white tongues that forked and darted at the edge of camp and at the cusp of a downward slope. The dune thicket fell to the shore carpeted with dense inkberries, and the fragrance of sea daisies rode up on the aether breeze mixing with the pines and the fires, and the moon was a pad of maple sugar that candled creaminess through sky and water. They saw its path of light through the only gap in the plant wall. Hemmed into the crowded plant community, the site was a lit mouth of space, and the sea wind came up and rustled the flora. Camp leaves nuzzled each other, and they heard the other plants all around, chitchatting with the wind that pushed through their midnight ruck.

"Have yall seen my crystal?" Manny said. "Hold on." He went inside the van and came back out cradling a dingy formation of rough shapes. He put it down on the wool blanket across the fire from where they all sat. "It helps the radio pick up a signal better," he said. "Watch this." Standing by the van, he extended the antenna of his boom box. The speakers blasted white noise. "Nothing, right? Now watch what happens when I bring it over and sit it by the crystal." Drums and electric guitar bumped in and took over the static sound. "See?" he said. Manny collapsed crossed-legged behind the crystal and the boom box, looking down, like watching them helped him hear the music better. "That's nice," he said. He had bought cans instead of bottles this time. One hissed and opened in his hand, and he took a long drink. "That's a good taste. Yall help yourself. It's nice to have company out here," he said, and he lay back and looked into the canopy of leaf undersides, tanning above the campfire. He was restless. He did a sit-up and got to his feet again, picking up a stick and walking over to the barrel fire. He swung it against the wall of plants and beat the brush back around the barrel. He stoked the fire with the jagged blond tip, and sparks rose up through the trees like warm confetti.

"Can we change the station?" Maunar said. "Or will the crystal mind?"

"Aw no, the crystal will play anything," Manny said. "As soon as this dies down, we'll put the grate over the top of the barrel and cook the hotdogs."

Maunar crawled across the blankets and limbs toward the crystal. She turned a wheel on the boom box. Hip hop beats merged with the rock music. She kept turning, and the hip hop won out. Maunar turned the volume up using the neighboring wheel.

"Does anybody want a beer?" Kyle said. He stepped over the limbs and walked under the canopy to the cooler.

"I'll take one."

"I'll take one."

"Just get everybody one," Manny yelled from the barrel fire. "Everybody wants one, right?"

"And could you bring the Skittles?" Honey said, sitting on the blanket, hugging her legs to her chest.

"We'll have Skittles as an appetizer," Maunar said.

"Hey, you laugh, but I've had those things as an entrée," Manny said. They laughed again. "More times than one."

They moved the crystal and the boom box back, and music battered out from under the tarp canopy. Heel boning on the wool blanket, Honey and Don moved together to the beat. Kyle sat on the blanket watching her figure working with the sounds, and her long sleek torso was hidden in the clothes she borrowed from him. They bundled around her best parts, her curvature lost somewhere inside the shapeless male cuts. She backed up to Don and shook. The slick gym shorts covered her knees and shimmered. Maunar laughed and clapped and looked at Kyle. "Come on," she said. "They got nothing," and they stood together on the blanket dancing and making a rivalry of the mismatch. The harlem shake in the middle of nowhere. Vibration traveled through them to different joints, and they rattled in place and warped themselves, dipping and grinding, locking and dropping, and the couples mixed. They all danced together on the wool blanket. Kyle bumped kinetic energy through himself and gestured on the blanket like an orchestra conductor. He tasted someone's hair. He touched Honey's waist. She was in a trance, and he heard Manny on the outside of the circle chanting a freestyle rap of elementary rhymes. "I once offered some beer to a giraffe. She said, no, she wanted wine from a carafe."

Kyle left the dance party and walked off by himself. Down the slope stepping on the coverage, he carried his beer and found a clear spot of loose sand to sit down in. He took long sips of his beer and looked out at the water. It rolled toward the land all the time, and the moon sat up there without giving him any ideas, and open night was black and silver like a picture negative. In a nest with the dune hedges thick around him, he dug his heels into the sand and felt the temperatures of daytime unearthed and rising to his calves. Party sounds came from the top of the dune, and he looked up at the career of the firelight. The pulsing dome pushed a glow into the mound of dark vegetation, and the lively cave was what he had just come from. He saw it small now from below. He didn't know the island. He didn't understand the island yet, and that was someone else's den on the dune top. The fist of light gripped the tangled growth. He belonged there for the night as Manny's guest, and he had evacuated his own place on the island. Other places had felt like they were his as soon as he had gotten to them, like they had been his all along. Panama City had been like that. Wing tabs buzzed in the bushes around him. He dug his heels in the slope, and the moon gave him no feelings to look at. He didn't recognize the moon. Its personality was different. It looked different over an island he didn't know, and he wanted to see the moon that rose over the neon strip in Panama City or the moon that came up through the pine islands at home. He took it out on his beer. Drinking it rough and sloppy, it creeked out of the corners of his mouth, and he felt a coolness soak into his shirt. He got the idea to bury something in the sand. He wanted to mark the nest and put a treasure in it that he could come back to when things were different, and he could start over with the island, maybe later on in life. He imagined coming back with children and a wife, blurred and faceless people. He reached in his pockets. He had keys that he needed to send back to Ernest, the hotel manager. He had change that could have belonged to anybody. He thought about the relics at the expensive restaurant he went to above the town, the old pirate toys, the tarnished silver. The rust was prettier than the relics in some cases. In the other pocket, he felt the designer sunglasses. They weren't his, and they didn't mean anything. He decided not to bury them. In the black bowl of water, he knew the marine animals were going crazy, fighting with eyes that saw in water and glowed with nocturnity, and every eye has its ideal situation, he thought. The bugs tattered through the leathery leaves all around him, zapping their backs into flight, and they seemed like true professionals in the inkberries. The moon was a lazy eye. Its crescent stare set towards the black mountain slope. He had nothing to bury.

The wire rack spanned the barrel fire and banded the hotdogs with char marks. Smoke spiraled through the grate in sheer windpipes, and Kyle walked back into the campsite. He circled the fire and sat down on a blanket. Honey sat next to Maunar. "You have such a beautiful complexion," she said. Can I touch your face?"

"Okay," Maunar said.

Honey leaned over her own crossed legs, and touched Maunar's cheek. She ran her hand down to her jawbone and traced it toward her chin. "It feels just like I thought it would. It looks like you have an undertone of butter." Honey dropped Skittles from her other hand, and they fell on the wool blanket. She picked them up, one by one, and put them in her mouth. Don straddled a limb and dragged more of it into the fire. Part of the blanket hung on a natural hook, and the blanket bunched and went toward the flames.

Maunar saw it and leaned back and freed the blanket. She pulled it away from the stones and warm conchs and straightened it back into place.

They ate bunless hotdogs and Skittles. The candy collected and coated his throat making it hard to swallow. Kyle took a sip of a new beer, and the cold tab touched his nose.

"I wish my little Amber were here," Maunar said. "She's my little kitten. We get along great together."

"Preshimay," Honey said.

"Little mauve-nosed Amber. If she were here, I'd give here a piece of hotdog on that warm conch, and then she'd go over there and bathe herself with her little pink tongue."

"The purple ones go best with the hotdogs," Kyle said.

"Pass the boy some purples, somebody." Honey passed him the bag.

"I was really just kidding," Kyle said. "I'll take some more though. Thank you." The package was slick, and the pellets of candy were chilled. Condensation coated them when he brought them into the night air, and they dyed his fingers. He ate whatever he pulled out, and he didn't really care about the colors. The Skittles were unfocused masses that he brought close to his face like pills. The blurs still had colors, and he made his hand a funnel and closed his eyes and put so many in at once, like overdosing on placebos. He couldn't tell what he was eating, and the hotdog meat dissolved in with the mixture.

"I think I'm going to stay up all night," Honey said. "We'll just have to get up again in like four more hours. It might be easier if we don't sleep at all."

"Let's do it," Manny said. He smoked his cigarette down to the filter and tossed the butt into the fire.

Kyle leaned back on his elbow. The wool blanket was scratchy to his skin, and he buried his face in the crook of his arm when the smoke floated his way. He stared into the fire. He had almost swallowed some fire the night before. He would have swallowed fire and taken in some of the island elements that way. The cracked-face joker-jumper had picked him out of the crowd and offered him a taste, and it had seemed appealing at the time. Manny's campfire didn't look edible like the fire breather's stabbed flame had. The fire breather's fire had been on a skewer like shish kabob, and Kyle thought of vegetables and fire and steak and rainbows, and all the things he had just eaten were taking over his brain and face, and he was dissolving, hypnotized by the fire. Low flames sat on the wood, waving purple and blue, undulating like the skirts of a mollusk, and looking at the hottest white part was like seeing so much of everything, every light and every color, but there was nothing there, and it was white nothing. He sat on the wool blanket comparing black nothing and white nothing. Both were there. The night behind him was black nothing. The bending flames in front of him were white nothing. He felt sleepy and boring like his mind was shot, and he didn't think he was fit to say anything else to anybody. He lost track of the ideas he made in his head. He didn't know what the outcome of the argument was, white nothing versus black nothing. He didn't know which was better. His mind was getting soft. His temples felt furry with warm blood, and he was bored with his own thoughts about colors.

He crawled into the back of Manny's van dragging one of the wool blankets with him. He lay down on the burgundy upholstery and covered himself using his knapsack as a pillow and lying on his side. He dragged the rolling suitcase next to him and propped one leg on it, and one arm hugged the luggage. He faded without jerking, and he started dreaming immediately. He saw an athlete with gold finger curls covering his head. He was slouched on a cloud. He asked every passing angel the whereabouts of his cleats, and they told him that cleats were earth things and he didn't need them anymore. He asked how he would run in the clouds, and they laughed at him. He thought it was a legitimate question, so he didn't laugh with them but asked what their problem was. The helpful angels told him to look down at his body. He looked down, but there was no body anymore. His spirit was naked. It floated under his head like a series of gold ropes. Honey straddled his sleeping body. The angels asked how he could wear cleats without feet or a body, and they laughed again. This time the athlete laughed, too. He dangled the gold soul ropes with his will power.

Kyle blinked in a tent of her long blond hair. It hung down, and she hugged his head, and her face came closer. She rubbed her nose all over his face, and he had the idea that she might love him. "I'll wake you up when we leave," she said. "I'll wake you up soon, Butter Bears."

"Kyle," she said. "Wake up. We're leaving. Do you remember when I blessed you?"

"I didn't know that's what you were doing."

"Your head just came up into my arms, and it floated like there was nothing attached to it," she said. "Do you remember that, when I blessed you? Were you awake enough?"

"Yeah, you just did it."

"No, Butters, that was about three hours ago. It felt like God was sitting inside me. The sun's about to come up now, and we're driving to the airport."

The van hummed over the Moravian Highway. Kyle felt warm morning air blowing in the open window through Manny's hair. He smelled the fire smoke and oils, and he lifted himself up on his arm. Maunar and Don swiveled in their chairs and looked down at him. Honey sat on the floor leaning against the van wall with the wind wrapping her hair across her face. "Butters, you're up, again" she said. "You can't stop sleeping." She pulled the hair down and squinted, and a strand stayed stuck in the corner of her mouth.

"She has butter on the mind," Maunar said.

"Makes me wish for breakfast," Don said.

"Why'd you call me Butters?"

"You've just been Butters," she said.

Kyle's spine tingled like he had woken up from a fever sleep, and he was confused, and the chemicals of night still flowed through his senses. His eyes were fogged over with sleep and thick, salted air. He heard bugs hitting the windshield, and a deep blue was just coming into the sky ahead of them. The tinted strip across the top of the windshield bruised the color darker, and the saturated blue looked expensive, the ultramarine of lapis lazuli, like the deep ocean he had just kicked against. The highway opened up to the water, and it was the same color as the sky, and they were surrounded by dawn diffusing through the cake of earth, and the bunt dome sucked light into its pores. They saw hints of genesis filtering down to them, buried under the lowest layers of the sky stack.

"I want a rich roll covered in eggs and sweetness," Don said.

"I want to breathe in powdered sugar off a slice of doughnut and suffocate," Maunar said.

"I want to burn my tongue with black coffee."

"I want to throw a pie in somebody's face," Honey said, and they all laughed.

"All yall've been up all night," Kyle said. His mouth felt thick, and his lips were swollen.

"His first joke of the day. You talked in your sleep again," Don said.

"I don't think you can call it talking," Honey said. "Unless there's a caveman interpreter around here somewhere."

Behind a line of safari taxis and burgundy transport vans, Manny parked parallel to the curb in front of the terminal. The sidewalk was already crowded with people and piles of luggage, and skycaps yelled out to the people, asking to porter their bags and check them in curbside. All the travelers were ruddy and clean from hot shower water. Honey jumped out of the van doors, and Kyle put his arms through the loops of his knapsack. He dragged his rolling suitcase out behind him and lifted it off the rear bumper, lowering it to the asphalt and extending the black handle. Honey stepped up onto the curb and crouched down in the middle of the foot traffic. Her hair tips swept the grimy concrete, and people took short steps on the balls of their feet to change their courses and avoid running into her. "Quick get something," she said.

"Get what?"

"Something to pick it up with."

A hermit crab stroked across the pavement hauling a curled seashell, banded with pastels. Kyle parked the suitcase upright and bent down next to Honey. The crab stopped and sucked some of itself back into the hollowed calyx. Its beard of legs and claws hung out of the opening, and its black eye nubs spied out against the turbo pearl of its interior shell. "We can't take it on the plane."

"I just want to move it so no one steps on it," she said. Kyle stood up and looked at the acres of parking lot around them, and he met faces with all of the oncoming people.

"I don't know. There's no where to put it, is there?"

Maunar crouched down next to the hermit crab, and Kyle rolled his suitcase out of her way and stood with Don. Don stretched, and Manny came over putting his shirt on and adjusting his medallions. The men stood in front of the sliding doors that opened and closed and opened again for people going into the terminal. They watched the women huddled by the curb, and looking east, haze heathered the teal sides of the mountains that faced them, and the sky grew more banded, tie-dyed, soaked with rays of color, and metallic trim bordered vast clouds that hung like the countries of heaven in the approaching light of sunrise. The row of terminal windows took the oncoming light and scattered it under the low roof of the steel portico. Maunar picked up the hermit crab's shell between her thumb and forefinger, and it scissored its jointed antennae, splayed its probes and swam in the air, hanging out of its shell. She walked with it and held her other hand below, cupped, like the drip-catcher that escorts a spoon-feeding, and she and the crab disappeared around a pebbled column. Honey followed. There was a lull in the foot traffic, but the automatic doors still parted on their tracks, and closed and opened again, and the black bristles underneath the door swept clear the grooves of the metal threshold.

"Are we causing that?" Don said.

Manny looked over his shoulder. "I think we might be," he said. "Let's scoot over this way."

Kyle rolled his suitcase, and they all took a few steps to their left, escaping the range of the trapezoidal black goggle that hung over the entryway detecting them.

Honey and Maunar came back around the pebbled column calling for a cup. "To hold the hermit crab. There isn't a good place to put it anywhere," Honey said. "Maunar can release it on the beach later."

"I have a cup." Manny opened the passenger-side door of his van and leaned inside. He brought out a plastic cup and handed it to Honey, and she put her nose inside. "Is this a used cup?"

"Used for beer. Yes it was, little girlfriend."

"You don't have a clean one, or can you wash this one out?"

"I think we'd better get inside," Kyle said. "This is a high profile area, and we're just standing around out here."

"The yeast smell won't bother it. Crabs are like sailors," Manny said.

"Cause they cuss?" Kyle said.

"It's a shame you're going home so soon, partner. We could've

104

gotten into some unusual stuff this summer. But, hey, I don't blame you." He leaned in sideways and gargled words from the corner of his mouth. "I'd go where that goes, too," he said, and Kyle followed his eyes toward Honey bending over in the slick fabric of his gym shorts.

"Yeah, my clothes do nothing for her," he said.

"I've always said, women look better without clothes, and men look better with them."

She tilted the used cup over on its side and put the hermit crab in front of it on the concrete to see whether it approved or not. With its plum of claw leading, the crab's vermillion leg blades swept the plastic side of the cup without traction, and it dragged the shell inside.

At the security line, Kyle lifted a gray tub from the stack and put it down on a stainless steel counter. Honey stepped backwards out of her flip flops. Heel and joint indentions blackened the pink foam, and Kyle put his tennis shoes in the tub and emptied his pockets. "I guess this is where we leave yall," Manny said. Kyle took his address book out of his knapsack and wrote down their addresses. "I'll send you thank you notes," he said. "I appreciate your helping me."

"Good luck," Maunar said.

She hugged Honey, and Honey handed over the plastic cup. The hermit crab was tucked up in its shell in the bottom. "I had fun last night and the night before, and it was nice meeting you, everybody."

Don shook hands with Kyle and pulled him in close. He said into his ear, "I hadn't had a chance to tell you I told you so," Don said.

"Saying that was good enough, I guess. You were dead on. Watch out for the iguanas." He handed Don his room keys. "Give those to Ernest, will you? And tell him I'm sorry."

"It happens," Don said. "Maybe another summer ten years down the road."

"That's what I was thinking," Kyle said. He took his knapsack off his shoulders, laid it flat on the conveyor belt behind their tub of shoes, change, the sunglasses, and everything disappeared into the metal x-ray booth through a curtain of rubber flaps. They were stripped down to clothes only. Honey had no pockets, and his were empty, and a limited thought line chased itself by the tail in his brain, and it was in the root language of people. He read the signs that guided him through the checkpoint, and they processed barefooted along the mat with gritty feet and sand sparkles stuck to their suntans, like feral children who grew tired of their wild wolf mothers, turning themselves over to authorities. The officer on the other side of the metal detector wore latex gloves. He held his palm up to them, and they stopped in front of the rectangular gantry. On his signal, they passed through, one at a time, ritualistic like druids through a sarsen stone gate. Kyle thought he might feel something walking through the metal detector. He imagined some alteration to his makeup, and he braced himself for the magnetic currents that would eddy through him. He passed through and didn't feel anything. He felt unchanged, and he nodded to the officer who signaled again with his latex glove. Honey approached the freestanding air door on her way to the secure side. She looked up at the alternating lights across the lintel and passed through the modern trilithon without a tone.

Airside, they walked through a short hall. Slick posters of local art, bordered with hunter-black margins and title footers, hung framed in plexiglass, and her flip-flops clapped between the tile and her heel. They held hands, and the straps of his knapsack's hip belt swung against the union. A group of retirees crowded a souvenir stand, browsing the items and daydreaming into the fluorescent lights, the tubes of excited vapor bent in their lenses, and bifocals magnified eyes that got lost in the loud colors of the slotted magazine wall. Decked in pied tropicality, the octogenarians modeled visors for each other, the plastic grips disappearing skull-wards through cirrus curls of whisked hair, and the wire postcard rack carouselled to the touch. The column of gorgeous beach edens and aqua fantasy lands revolved. He wanted to hold the scenes. The clear water looked good. Even when he had actually stood on the beach, he wanted something from it that he couldn't explain. He wanted to have paradise inside his body somehow. He wanted the blue waters to replace his blood. Maybe the aristocrats were sea-veined, he thought, and the fountain of youth was always more about a marriage to pure beauty than it was living forever. The water had fallen through his hands. Hugging the sea felt like hugging nothing, and rebirths were always more memorable than first births. Just having been there for three weeks wasn't enough. Nothing of him was fused with the genius of St. Thomas. There had been glimpses, but he wasn't satisfied. He lacked a sense of nativity for the place, and for the first time, pictures seemed like a good idea to him. The photos held more of the island's aura than he had absorbed, and he thought of stopping to buy a few. They were four for a dollar, but the intercom came on again giving news of rows past theirs already boarding. They moved on through the concourse toward the gates.

They got in line. A small airport, all the gates were together at ground level, and families camped in rows of siamese chairs joined at the armrests. Children rolled in the floor. Picture windows looked out across the tarmac where moveable staircases drove from plane to plane and polished jet bellies lay prone on their wheel assemblies. A line of travelers disembarked, and mesh-vested ushers waved them through a course of cones toward the building. Inside, they amassed at the welcome booth where costumed islanders served free cups of bright coral rum drinks, and a thin man banged a handheld dish gong. "Look at these idiots. Why are people drinking so early in the morning?" Honey said.

"For all we know, it could be midnight where they're coming from."

An alcove housed a horseshoe of food court, and curved neon spelling hung on the tile. Zataurus sat alone at a round table. No posse in sight, his head was bowed low. His shoulder blades boned through the back of his white suit, and his finger and thumb excavated the inner crumb cliffs of a huge blueberry muffin in front of him on the table. He stared into the muffin. Standing in line, Kyle saw him first. He gripped his boarding pass and stared. The blueberries were cobalt, and the muffin was a development of bread that rose enormous from a flattened circle of cupcake paper. A ceramic travel mug, filled with coffee, steamed without a lid. Everything Kyle saw tricked him and gave him tunnel vision. He couldn't believe it. The shot tracked forward and zoomed out at the same time, so the backdrop of the muffin crowded around, and he felt like it was the one true thing in the terminal dawn. The sassy muffin lip was an erotic cleft between the swelling smoothness of the golden cap and the gritty form-fitting base, and it sat steadfast in the space it held, saying nothing about being a muffin, but the room knew it was one by the way it held itself, soaking the food court light into its baked-good shape, and the blond cake was saturated with the blue blood of cooked berries. It asked to give to tongue and face, and it begged for Kyle's stares, and he gave them, unable to look anywhere else, not knowing what to do.

The line advanced, and they shuffled closer toward the woman at the gate. Her cheeks looked caught in the smile she wore, and she tore tabs from the boarding passes along lines of perforation. Kyle inched along. Honey didn't move, and he felt her notice Zataurus. Kyle looked back, and a triangle of seeing developed among the three of them. Each set of eyeballs twitched back and forth between the other two points, and they became aware of each other at the same time. Zataurus eased his forearms off the table and sat back in his chair. He looked around at the people filing into the concourse, and with his index and middle fingers coupled like a gun barrel, he made two sharp sweeps toward himself, calling for her to come to him. The boarding line advanced, and they took another step forward. Honey looked at Kyle, and he could tell there was something inside her that pulled toward Zataurus. Stolid like a teak idol in the food court, his pull was natural, and he drew the energy in the room toward him like a draft. She sucked on the inside of her mouth trying to form the words that could break what she wanted to say with grace, and some sort of remorse panged around behind her face.

"We just met."

"It felt natural," he said.

"We started talking in the bar like we had left off from some earlier conversation."

"But we don't really know each other, right?"

A searching look touched her eyes, and a tightness in her top lip contorted her funny mouth in a new way. She looked at Zataurus again and tucked her hair behind her ear.

"Just keep your eyes open for a girl named Sabine," she said. "She lives in Florida. She looks just like me."

Honey lowered her head and put her hand on his shoulder. She walked past him dragging her fingers across his chest. The line moved forward again, and he watched her move through the crowd. The airline attendant smiled, welcomed him to the flight and ripped the stub off his ticket. He turned around beside the propped-open glass doors, and the man behind him in line was close and in his face. The concourse was filled with people.

A deep coffee stain bothered the stripes of a man's seersucker shorts. Kyle watched him go up on his toes to stuff his luggage in the overhead bin, and his shirt was tucked in tight. Everyone sat down, and no new people came down the aisles. Only the flight attendants cruised like high-minded pumas, giving effleurage to the seatbacks. Kyle let himself have the window, and his knapsack rode beside him in the aisle seat. He looked out behind the wing, unable to see the engines, but he heard them revving out of their warm-up whines into deep barrel tones, and the plane started to taxi. The terminal swung into view. All the picture windows showed black in the building umbra, and the shadow of the winglet stretched in the low sunlight and swung toward his porthole. A flight attendant bent down and slapped his tray flush with the seat in front of him, and his legs were exposed. Gray ravels from his cutoffs lay across the sun-bleached leg hair on his tan knees, and he heard the operation of electronics under his feet. The flaps elevated and dropped camber-flush with the foil again. The equipment tested true, and at the end of the runway, everything went still. The plane seemed to park. The idle engines hummed. Then the gunning sucked the sound from the cabin, and he was pressed into his seat. The plane jetted down the runway, and then he was weightless. He flew through dawn. The plane angled into the heavens and flew from the island.

Out over the water, they banked hard. A fuzzy brightness went by the double-paned window, and the sun was bloated in all the atmosphere it came through. It busted through the oval of its squat morning sphere, and the bright apricot was hard to see in the bright apricot sky. The plane kept its slant. The island came into the panes. He saw the whole thing from above. Bearded slopes rode turquoise shelves that drowned in the shallows, and the land chain junked up the smooth smear of sea. They spiraled higher, and the place looked small and make-believe, and fresh memories played through his head like the details of a story that happened to someone else a long time ago. The plane bucked through layers of water smoke until the clouds stacked below like three-dimensional projections of white rock. Sky tumbled through the canisters of engine under the wings, and the change in pressure hushed everything in his ears. He plugged his headphones into the armrest jack and scrolled through the in-flight stations. The reggae cruised. Locked into a west-northwestern course, the plane leveled off and chased the night. The altitude showed a dimness in the distance that he had already lived through, and he felt like sleeping again.

Across the aisles, the opposite, fresh sunlight came into the plane, and a girl's diamond ring saw more of the future. Its facets organized the light into a dozen thrown parts. The girl didn't see the display or know she had any part in it. She wrung her hands in her lap. Kyle leaned his head back on the seat's headrest, watching the scatter of spectrums shake on the cabin wall.

www.ingramcontent.com/pod-product-compliance
Lightning Source LLC
Chambersburg PA
CBHW020630250626
47154CB00004B/1748